I REMEMBER,
I REMEMBER

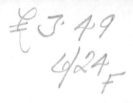

I REMEMBER,
I REMEMBER

Illustrated by
Trevor Newton

Compiled by Rob Farrow
Edited by Jennifer Curry

RED FOX

3 4 7 9 10 8 6 4 2

Copyright text in this collection
© The Malcolm Sargent Cancer Fund 1993

Copyright © illustrations
Trevor Newton 1993

Trevor Newton has asserted his right under the Copyright,
Designs and Patents Act, 1988 to be identified as the
illustrator of this work

For individual copyright, see the acknowledgments of
poets page which constitutes an extension of the
copyright notice

First published in the United Kingdom 1993
by The Bodley Head Children's Books
Random House, 20 Vauxhall Bridge Road
London SW1V 2SA

Random House Autralia (Pty) Limited
20 Alfred Street, Milsons Point, Sydney
New South Wales 2061, Australia

Random House New Zealand Limited
18 Poland Road, Glenfield,
Auckland 10, New Zealand

Random House South Africa (Pty) Limited
PO Box 337, Bergvlei 2012, South Africa

Random House UK Limited
Reg. No. 954009

A CIP catalogue record for this book is available from
the British Library

ISBN 0 370 31909 5

Printed and bound in Great Britain by
Cox & Wyman Ltd, Reading, Berkshire

Set in Goudy
Printed and bound in Great Britain
by Cox & Wyman Ltd, Reading, Berks

RANDOM HOUSE UK Limited Reg. No. 954009

ISBN 0 09 931831 8

Contents

Part 2 THE GENTLEMEN GO BY
Poems About People

Part 3 **AWAY DOWN THE VALLEY,
AWAY DOWN THE HILL**
Poems About Travelling

Part 4 I HAVE FOUGHT SUCH A FIGHT
Poems of War and Peace

Part 5 VELVET TIGERS AND MEEK MILD CREATURES
Poems of Birds and Beasts

Part 6 LOOK UP AT THE SKIES
Poems of the Weather and Seasons

Part 7 A FIRE WAS IN MY HEAD
Poems of Magic and Mystery

Part 8 STUMBLING BLOCKS AND STEPPING STONES
Poems About Life, Death and Being

'I Remember . . .'

. . . a Dedication

To all children smitten by some shape of cancer and to Adam, Annabel, Harriet, Sebastian & Simon-Luc who are lucky in that they are not.
The purpose of this book is to raise money for the Malcolm Sargent Cancer Fund for children, a charity which has, for twenty-five years, given succour and support to children, and the families of children, suffering from this unspeakable disease.
  The initiative, the momentum and much of the wherewithal for the assembling of this anthology are the gift of Fergus and Vivian Falk. Other sponsors, some of whom are listed below, have been extremely generous.

Dannie Abse
Allan Ahlberg
Brian Aldiss
Kenneth Baker
Jill Barklem
Rabbi Lionel Blue
Raymond Briggs
Dame Elizabeth Butler-Sloss
Lord Carrington
Helen Cresswell
Dr Cyril Cusack
Colin Dann
Sir Peter de la Billiere
Len Deighton
Dame Mary Donaldson
Margaret Drabble
Dr Charles Farncombe
Finers Solicitors
Paul Gascoigne
Sir John Gielgud
Susan Hampshire
Sir Nigel Hawthorne
Bob Holness
Glenys Kinnock
David Kossoff

Hugh Laurie
Sue Lawley
Patrick Leigh Fermor
John Lever
Bernard Levin
George MacDonald Fraser
John Julius Norwich
Matthew Parris
Kathleen Peyton (KM Peyton)
Judge James Pickles
Marjorie Proops
Frederick Raphael
Vernon Scannell
Posy Simmonds
Sir Clive Sinclair
Jon Snow
Graham Taylor
Lord Taylor of Gosforth
Norman Thelwell
Dorothy Tutin
Sir Peter Ustinov
Chad Varah
Baroness Warnock
Mary Whitehouse
JA Wright (James Herriot)

Part 1

UNDER THE APPLE BOUGHS
Poems of Place

Moonlit Apples
by John Drinkwater

At the top of the house the apples are laid in rows,
And the skylight lets the moonlight in, and those
Apples are deep-sea apples of green. There goes
  A cloud on the moon in the autumn night.

A mouse in the wainscot scratches, and scratches, and
    then
There is no sound at the top of the house of men
Or mice; and the cloud is blown, and the moon again
    Dapples the apples with deep-sea light.

They are lying in rows there, under the gloomy beams;
On the sagging floor; they gather the silver streams
Out of the moon, those moonlit apples of dreams,
    And quiet is the steep stair under.

In the corridors under there is nothing but sleep.
And stiller than ever on orchard boughs they keep
Tryst with the moon, and deep is the silence, deep
    On moon-washed apples of wonder.

Chosen by **Dame Muriel Spark**, novelist, whose works include *The Prime of
Miss Jean Brodie*

❛*Moonlit Apples* has always appealed to me for its atmosphere
– like an Impressionist painting. There is a magic in this poem
that reaches beyond the actual picture evoked.❜

The Listeners

by Walter de la Mare

'Is there anybody there?' said the Traveller,
    Knocking on the moonlit door;
And his horse in the silence champ'd the grasses
    Of the forest's ferny floor:
And a bird flew up out of the turret,
    Above the Traveller's head:
And he smote upon the door again a second time;
    'Is there anybody there?' he said.

But no one descended to the Traveller;
    No head from the leaf-fringed sill.
Lean'd over and look'd into his grey eyes,
    Where he stood perplex'd and still.
But only a host of phantom listeners
    That dwelt in the lone house then
Stood listening in the quiet of the moonlight
    To that voice from the world of men:
Stood thronging the faint moonbeams on the dark stair,
    That goes down to the empty hall,
Hearkening in an air stirr'd and shaken
    By the lonely Traveller's call.
And he felt in his heart their strangeness,
    Their stillness answering his cry,
While his horse moved, cropping the dark turf,
    'Neath the starrred and leafy sky;
For he suddenly smote on the door, even
    Louder, and lifted his head: —
'Tell them I came, and no one answered,
    That I kept my word,' he said.
Never the least stir made the listeners,
    Though every word he spake
Fell echoing through the shadowiness of the still house
    From the one man left awake:
Ay, they heard his foot upon the stirrup,
    And the sound of iron on stone,
And how the silence surged softly backward,
    When the plunging hoofs were gone.

Chosen by **Michael McCrum**, Master of Corpus Christi College, Cambridge

❟This was one of the first poems I learnt at school. It has a haunting quality. Who is the mysterious Traveller? Whom was he hoping to find? Why did they not answer his question, which they heard so clearly? Is the Traveller you or me trying to get into touch with a spiritual world?❠

I Remember, I Remember

by Thomas Hood

I remember, I remember,
The house where I was born,
The little window where the sun
Came peeping in at morn;
He never came a wink too soon,
Nor brought too long a day,
But now, I often wish the night
Had borne my breath away!

I remember, I remember,
The roses, red and white,
The violets, and the lily-cups,
Those flowers made of light!
The lilacs where the robin built,
And where my brother set
The laburnum on his birthday,—
The tree is living yet!

I remember, I remember,
Where I was used to swing,
And thought the air must rush as fresh
To swallows on the wing;
My spirit flew in feathers then,
That is so heavy now,
And summer pools could hardly cool
The fever on my brow!

I remember, I remember,
The fir trees dark and high;
I used to think their slender tops
Were close against the sky:
It was a childish ignorance,
But now 'tis little joy
To know I'm farther off from heaven
Than when I was a boy.

Chosen by **Matthew Parris**, humorist, author, journalist and broadcaster

❛Adults often pretend they liked in childhood what, really, they like now. This poem I did like. As a teenager I thought it very true, and sad.❜

The Watchers

by Edward Thomas

By the ford at the town's edge
Horse and carter rest:
The carter smokes on the bridge
Watching the water press in swathes about his horse's
    chest.

From the inn one watches, too,
In the room for visitors
That has no fire, but a view
And many cases of stuffed fish, vermin, and kingfishers.

Chosen by **Raymond Briggs**, children's author and illustrator, whose works
include *The Snowman* and, most recently, *The Man*

‛It is visually very clear, with an almost film-like vividness. It
also has a feeling of peace, stillness and quiet, representing
a world which has gone for ever.’

Fern Hill

by Dylan Thomas

Now as I was young and easy under the apple boughs
About the lilting house and happy as the grass was green,
    The night above the dingle starry,
      Time let me hail and climb
    Golden in the heydays of his eyes,
And honoured among wagons I was prince of the apple
        towns
And once below a time I lordly had the trees and leaves
      Trail with daisies and barley
    Down the rivers of the windfall light.

And as I was green and carefree, famous among the
     barns
About the happy yard and singing as the farm was
          home,
   In the sun that is young once only,
        Time let me play and be
   Golden in the mercy of his means,
And green and golden I was huntsman and herdsman,
          the calves
Sang to my horn, the foxes on the hills barked clear
     and cold
        And the sabbath rang slowly
   In the pebbles of the holy streams.

All the sun long it was running, it was lovely, the hay
Fields high as the house, the tunes from the chimneys,
          it was air
     And playing, lovely and watery
        And fire green as grass.
     And nightly under the simple stars
As I rode to sleep the owls were bearing the farm away,
All the moon long I heard, blessed among stables, the
          night-jars
     Flying with the ricks, and the horses
        Flashing into the dark.

And then to awake, and the farm, like a wanderer white
With the dew, come back, the cock on his shoulder: it
          was all
   Shining, it was Adam and maiden,
        The sky gathered again
   And the sun grew round that very day.
So it must have been after the birth of the simple light
In the first, spinning place, the spellbound horses
          walking warm
     Out of the whinnying green stable.

And honoured among foxes and pheasants by the gay
            house
Under the new made clouds and happy as the heart
            was long,
    In the sun born over and over,
        I ran my heedless ways,
    My wishes raced through the house high hay
And nothing I cared, at my sky blue trades, that time
            allows
In all his tuneful turning so few and such morning songs
        Before the children green and golden
            Follow him out of grace.

Nothing I cared, in the lamb white days, that time
            would take me
Up to the swallow thronged loft by the shadow of my
            hand,
        In the moon that is always rising,
            Nor that riding to sleep
        I should hear him fly with the high fields
And wake to the farm forever fled from the childless
            land.
Oh as I was young and easy in the mercy of his means,
        Time held me green and dying
        Though I sang in my chains like the sea.

Chosen by **Norman Thelwell**, artist and cartoonist

❲I was born in Birkenhead, very close to the countryside of
the Wirral and just a bicycle ride from North Wales. My
childhood seemed full of fields, farms, hills and wide
landscapes.
    Dylan Thomas's *Fern Hill* encapsulates the heady delights of
childhood for me when I too was young and easy under the
apple boughs.❳

Daffodils

by William Wordsworth

I wandered lonely as a cloud
   That floats on high o'er vales and hills,
When all at once I saw a crowd,
   A host, of golden daffodils;
Beside the lake, beneath the trees,
Fluttering and dancing in the breeze.

Continuous as the stars that shine
   And twinkle on the Milky Way,
They stretched in never-ending line
   Along the margin of a bay:
Ten thousand saw I at a glance,
Tossing their heads in sprightly dance.

The waves beside them danced, but they
   Out-did the sparkling waves in glee:
A poet could not but be gay,
   In such a jocund company:
I gazed—and gazed—but little thought
What wealth the show to me had brought:

For oft, when on my couch I lie
   In vacant or in pensive mood,
They flash upon that inward eye
   Which is the bliss of solitude;
And then my heart with pleasure fills,
And dances with the daffodils.

Chosen by **Susan Hampshire**, actress

❛It was one of the first poems that I remember having read to
me. Then later, at school, it was part of our English lessons.
I loved, even at a very young age, the images it conjured up,
and also the closeness to nature.❜

The Glory of the Garden

by Rudyard Kipling

Our England is a garden that is full of stately views,
Of borders, beds and shrubberies and lawns and avenues,
With statues on the terraces and peacocks strutting by;
But the Glory of the Garden lies in more than meets
    the eye.

For where the old thick laurels grow, along the thin red
    wall,
You find the tool- and potting-sheds which are the heart
    of all;
The cold-frames and the hot-houses, the dungpits and
    the tanks,The rollers, carts and drain-pipes, with
    the barrows and the planks.

And there you'll see the gardeners, the men and
        'prentice boys
Told off to do as they are bid and do it without noise;
For, except when seeds are planted and we shout to
        scare the birds,
The Glory of the Garden it abideth not in words.

And some can pot begonias and some can bud a rose,
And some are hardly fit to trust with anything that grows;
But they can roll and trim the lawns and sift the sand
        and loam,
For the Glory of the Garden occupieth all who come.

Our England is a garden, and such gardens are not made
By singing:—'Oh, how beautiful!' and sitting in the
        shade,
While better men than we go out and start their
        working lives
At grubbing weeds from gravel-paths with broken
        dinner-knives.

There's not a pair of legs so thin, there's not a head so
        thick,
There's not a hand so weak and white, nor yet a heart
        so sick,
But it can find some needful job that's crying to be done,
        For the Glory of the Garden glorifieth everyone.

Then seek your job with thankfulness and work till
        further orders,
If it's only netting strawberries or killing slugs on
        borders;
And when your back stops aching and your hands begin
        to harden,
You will find yourself a partner in the Glory of the
        Garden.

Oh, Adam was a gardener, and God who made him
    sees
That half a proper gardener's work is done upon his
    knees,
So when your work is finished, you can wash your hands
    and pray
For the Glory of the Garden, that it may not pass away!
And the Glory of the Garden it shall never pass away!

Chosen by Baroness Thatcher of Kesteven, better known as **Margaret Thatcher**, former Prime Minister

Buckingham Palace

by A.A. Milne

They're changing guard at Buckingham Palace—
Christopher Robin went down with Alice.
Alice is marrying one of the guard.
'A soldier's life is terrible hard,'
                Says Alice.

They're changing guard at Buckingham Palace—
Christopher Robin went down with Alice.
We saw a guard in a sentry-box.
'One of the sergeants looks after their socks,'
                Says Alice.

They're changing guard at Buckingham Palace—
Christopher Robin went down with Alice.
We looked for the King, but he never came.
'Well, God take care of him, all the same,'
                Says Alice.

They're changing guard at Buckingham Palace—
Christopher Robin went down with Alice.
They've great big parties inside the grounds.
'I wouldn't be King for a hundred pounds,'
Says Alice.

They're changing guard at Buckingham Palace—
Christopher Robin went down with Alice.
A face looked out, but it wasn't the King's.
'He's much too busy a-signing things,'
Says Alice.

They're changing guard at Buckingham Palace—
Christopher Robin went down with Alice.
'Do you think the King knows all about *me*?'
'Sure to, dear, but it's time for tea,'
Says Alice.

Chosen by **Rabbi Lionel Blue**, broadcaster and writer

❛Coming from an East End childhood I loved reading about nannies and high-class kids. Very exotic!❜

Hush! Hush!
by J.B. Morton

Hush! hush!
Nobody cares;
Christopher Robin
Has fallen downstairs.

Chosen by **Bernard Levin**, author, journalist and broadcaster

The Sacred Road

by *Idris Davies*

They walked this road in seasons past
When all the skies were overcast,
They breathed defiance as they went
Along those troubled hills of Gwent.

They talked of justice as they strode
Along this crooked mountain road,
And dared the little Lords of Hell
So that the future should be well.

Because they did not count the cost
But battled on when all seemed lost,
This empty ragged road shall be
Always a sacred road to me.

Chosen by the **Rt Hon Neil Kinnock** MP, former Leader of the Labour Party

Inversnaid

by *Gerard Manley Hopkins*

This darksome burn, horseback brown,
His rollrock highroad roaring down,
In coop and in comb the fleece of his foam
Flutes and low to the lake falls home.

A windpuff-bonnet of fawn-froth
Turns and twindles over the broth
Of a pool so pitchblack, fell-frowning,
It round and rounds Despair to drowning.

28

Degged with dew, dappled with dew
Are the groins of the braes that the brook treads
    through,
Wiry heathpacks, flitches of fern,
And the beadbonny ash that sits over the burn.

What would the world be, once bereft
Of wet and of wildness? Let them be left,
O let them be left, wildness and wet;
Long live the weeds and the wilderness yet.

Chosen by the **Rt Hon John Smith** QC MP, Leader of the Labour Party

❛I am a fan of Gerard Manley Hopkins and this poem has
some beautiful lines on the wet and wild places I love.❜

Dover Beach

by Matthew Arnold

The sea is calm to-night,
The tide is full, the moon lies fair
Upon the Straits;—on the French coast, the light
Gleams, and is gone; the cliffs of England stand,
Glimmering and vast, out in the tranquil bay.
Come to the window, sweet is the night air!
Only, from the long line of spray
Where the ebb meets the moon-blanch'd sand,
Listen! you hear the grating roar

Of pebbles which the waves suck back, and fling,
At their return, up the high strand,
Begin and cease, and then again begin,
With tremulous cadence slow, and bring
The eternal note of sadness in.

Sophocles long ago
Heard it on the Aegaean, and it brought
Into his mind the turbid ebb and flow
Of human misery; we
Find also in the sound a thought,
Hearing it by this distant northern sea.

The sea of faith
Was once, too, at the full, and round earth's shore
Lay like the folds of a bright girdle furl'd;
But now I only hear
Its melancholy, long withdrawing roar,
Retreating to the breath
Of the night-wind down the vast edges drear
And naked shingles of the world.

Ah, love, let us be true
To one another! for the world, which seems
To lie before us like a land of dreams,
So various, so beautiful, so new,
Hath really neither joy, nor love, nor light,
Nor certitude, nor peace, nor help for pain;
And we are here as on a darkling plain
Swept with confused alarms of struggle and flight,
Where ignorant armies clash by night.

Chosen by **Lord Taylor of Gosforth**, Lord Chief Justice; and **Sue Lawley**,
television and radio presenter of programmes including *Desert Island Discs*

❝I could choose many of Arnold's poems which formed the
first poetry to move me. *Dover Beach* is a wonderful evocation
of standing lonely on a beach and allowing the sand of the sea
to sweep into your mind.❞

  Sue Lawley

Tall Nettles

by Edward Thomas

Tall nettles cover up, as they have done
These many springs, the rusty harrow, the plough
Long worn out, and the roller made of stone:
Only the elm butt tops the nettles now.

This corner of the farmyard I like most:
As well as any bloom upon a flower
I like the dust on the nettles, never lost
Except to prove the sweetness of a shower.

Chosen by **J.K. Lever**, former cricketer for England and Essex.

31

Part 2

THE GENTLEMEN GO BY
Poems About People

The Thousandth Man
by Rudyard Kipling

One man in a thousand, Solomon says,
Will stick more close than a brother.
And it's worth while seeking him half your days
If you find him before the other.
Nine hundred and ninety-nine depend
On what the world sees in you,
But the Thousandth Man will stand your friend
With the whole round world agin you.

'Tis neither promise nor prayer nor show
Will settle the finding for 'ee.
Nine hundred and ninety-nine of 'em go
By your looks, or your acts, or your glory.
But if he finds you and you find him,
The rest of the world don't matter;
For the Thousandth Man will sink or swim
With you in any water.

You can use his purse with no more talk
Than he uses yours for his spendings,
And laugh and meet in your daily walk
As though there had been no lendings.
Nine hundred and ninety-nine of 'em call
For silver and gold in their dealings;
But the Thousandth Man he's worth 'em all,
Because you can show him your feelings.

His wrong's your wrong, and his right's your right,
In season or out of season.
Stand up and back it in all men's sight—
With *that* for your only reason!
Nine hundred and ninety-nine can't bide
The shame or mocking or laughter,
But the Thousandth Man will stand by your side
To the gallows-foot—and after!

Chosen by **Jeffrey Archer**, politician and bestselling novelist

Algernon

Who played with a Loaded Gun, and, on missing his Sister, was Reprimanded by his Father

by Hilaire Belloc

Young Algernon, the Doctor's Son,
Was playing with a Loaded Gun.
He pointed it towards his sister,
Aimed very carefully, but Missed her!
His Father, who was standing near,
The Loud Explosion chanced to Hear,
And reprimanded Algernon
For playing with a Loaded Gun.

Chosen by **James Hunt**, racing driver and television broadcaster

❛I thoroughly enjoyed this poem when I was a child and have recited it to my own children, giving much pleasure to me and them.❜

The Boy Stood On. . .

by Spike Milligan

The boy stood on the burning deck.
Twit.

Chosen by **David Gower** OBE, English Cricketer

❛This poem had the great qualities of being (a) short; so (b) memorable; and (c) succinct.❜

Jim,

Who ran away from his Nurse, and was eaten by a lion

by Hilaire Belloc

There was a Boy whose name was Jim;
His Friends were very good to him.
They gave him Tea, and Cakes, and Jam,
And slices of delicious Ham,
And Chocolate with pink inside,
And little Tricycles to ride,
And read him Stories through and through,
And even took him to the Zoo—
But there it was the dreadful Fate
Befell him, which I now relate.

You know—at least you *ought* to know,
For I have often told you so—
That Children never are allowed
To leave their Nurses in a Crowd;
Now this was Jim's especial Foible,
He ran away when he was able,
And on this inauspicious day
He slipped his hand and ran away!
He hadn't gone a yard when—

                         Bang!

    With open Jaws, a Lion sprang,
And hungrily began to eat
The Boy: beginning at his feet.
Now just imagine how it feels
When first your toes and then your heels,
And then by gradual degrees,
Your shins and ankles, calves and knees,
Are slowly eaten, bit by bit.

No wonder Jim detested it!
No wonder that he shouted 'Hi!'
The Honest Keeper heard his cry,
Though very fat he almost ran
To help the little gentleman.
'Ponto!' he ordered as he came
(For Ponto was the Lion's name),
'Ponto!' he cried, with angry Frown.
'Letgo, Sir! Down, Sir! Put it down!'

The Lion made a sudden Stop,
He let the Dainty Morsel drop,
And slunk reluctant to his Cage,
Snarling with Disappointed Rage
But when he bent him over Jim,
The Honest Keeper's Eyes were dim.
The Lion having reached his Head,
The Miserable Boy was dead!

When Nurse informed his Parents, they
Were more Concerned than I can say:—
His Mother, as She dried her eyes,
Said, 'Well—it gives me no surprise,
He would not do as he was told!'
His Father, who was self-controlled,
Bade all the children round attend
To James' miserable end,
And always keep a-hold of Nurse
For fear of finding something worse.

Chosen by **The Rt Hon Virginia Bottomley** MP, Secretary of State for Health

❮I remember this particular poem as one of my daughters recited it from beginning to end at the age of four.❯

One Funny Little Boy

Anon

I have one funny little boy
He comes up to my knee
He is the funniest little boy
Ever you did see.
He runs, he jumps, he smashes things
In all parts of the house
But what of that?
He is my son
My little Johann Strauss.

Chosen by **Pete Murray**, disc jockey

❝I have selected this poem purely and simply as it is one taught to me as a child and I've never forgotten it. I used to recite it with a German accent—and still do!❞

Sarah Byng

Who Could Not Read and was Tossed into a Thorny Hedge by a Bull

by Hilaire Belloc

Some years ago you heard me sing
My doubts on Alexander Byng.
His sister Sarah now inspires
My jaded Muse, my failing fires.
Of Sarah Byng the tale is told
How when the child was twelve years old
She could not read or write a line.
Her sister Jane, though barely nine,
Could spout the Catechism through
And parts of Matthew Arnold too,
While little Bill who came between

Was quite unnaturally keen
On 'Athalie', by Jean Racine.
But not so Sarah! Not so Sal!
She was a most uncultured girl
Who didn't care a pinch of snuff
For any literary stuff
And gave the classics all a miss.
Observe the consequence of this!
As she was walking home one day,
Upon the fields across her way
A gate, securely padlocked, stood,
And by its side a piece of wood
On which was painted plain and full,
BEWARE THE VERY FURIOUS BULL
Alas! The young illiterate
Went blindly forward to her fate,
And ignorantly climbed the gate!
Now happily the Bull that day
Was rather in the mood for play
Than goring people through and through
As Bulls so very often do;
He tossed her lightly with his horns
Into a prickly hedge of thorns,
And stood by laughing while she strode
And pushed and struggled to the road.
The lesson was not lost upon
The child, who since has always gone
A long way round to keep away
From signs, whatever they may say,
And leaves a padlocked gate alone.
Moreover she has wisely grown
Confirmed in her instinctive guess
That literature breeds distress.

Chosen by **John Julius Norwich**, writer, anthologist and broadcaster

❛I think Belloc the best comic poet in the English language.❜

The Brewer's Man

by L.A.G. Strong

Have I a wife? Bedam I have!
But we was badly mated.
I hit her a great clout one night,
And now we're separated.
And mornings going to me work
I meets her on the quay:
'Good mornin' to ye, ma'am!' says I,
'To hell with ye!' says she.

Chosen by **Robert Robinson**, writer, broadcaster and *Call My Bluff*
quizmaster

❛As a child I thought this verse was clever and funny and in
some way very pleasant. I thought that when I grew up and
went out into the world I should like to be among people who
were sharp and accurate like Strong, but also like Strong,
ironic and kind.❜

The Lamplighter

by Robert Louis Stevenson

My tea is nearly ready and the sun has left the sky;
It's time to take the window to see Leerie going by;
For every night at tea-time and before you take your
     seat,
With lantern and with ladder he comes posting up the
     street.

Now Tom would be a driver and Maria go to sea,
And my papa's a banker and as rich as he can be;
But I, when I am stronger and can choose what I'm to do,
O Leerie, I'll go round at night and light the lamps with
    you!

For we are very lucky, with a lamp before the door,
And Leerie stops to light it as he lights so many more;
And O! before you hurry by with ladder and with light,
O Leerie, see a little child and nod to him to-night!

Chosen by **Richard Baker** OBE, television and radio music broadcaster, and
former newscaster

❲When I was a child, I often stayed with my grandmother in
her Victorian house in Paddington. There was a gas lamp outside
the door which was lit every winter evening about teatime by
a man we identified as "Leerie the Lamplighter". I was very
fond of Stevenson's poem then, and I still am.❳

from A Smuggler's Song

by Rudyard Kipling

If you wake at midnight and hear a horse's feet,
Don't go drawing back the blind, or looking in the street,
Them that asks no questions isn't told a lie.
Watch the wall, my darling, while the Gentlemen go by!
Five and twenty ponies
Trotting through the dark—
Brandy for the Parson
Baccy for the Clerk;
Laces for a lady, letters for a spy,
Watch the wall, my darling, while the Gentlemen go by!

Chosen by **Sue Cook**, journalist, broadcaster and presenter of *Children in Need*

❛I was eleven years old, a first-year at my local grammar school, when the English teacher read *A Smuggler's Song* to the class. As a child I spent a lot of time in a dream world of my own and this poem gave me plenty of scope for fantasies. I used to think about the words at night in the darkness of my bedroom as I watched for the occasional beams of light which flickered across the ceiling whenever a car passed outside. If there was a bright moon, its light would shine through the ventilator brick, casting a row of pale circles on the opposite wall.

And as I watched my wall, I pondered on these dark adult intrigues and vices—baccy and brandy and secret messages. . . I wasn't sure what any of them were but I relished the dim sense of danger.

What if you DID look out of the window and see what you weren't supposed to see? And what were these adults up to? They were so secretive about their own lives and yet they still expected us kids to do as we were told!

Two years later, I had more pleasure from the poem. I remember singing it as a member of the school choir.❜

Just Me

by Paul Gascoigne

I'm a professional footballer
lying in a hospital bed
thinking of all those nasty things
all going through my head

I know I should not be lying here
it's because of Wembley
thinking of that stupid tackle
instead of all that glee

Now when I do get out of here
I'll be working on this knee
getting fit left, right and centre
just thinking of Italy

Now what is in my mind right now
no one will ever know
but when I'm given that big, big chance
it will be a one man show

Now Mel and Len both work for me
both working day and night
one's an accountant, one's a lawyer
making sure I'm alright

Now please don't worry about a thing
I know I'm getting thinner
but at the back of my mind
there'll only be one winner

Chosen by **Paul Gascoigne**, footballer for England and Lazio

Instead of choosing a favourite poem from his childhood, Paul
Gascoigne has contributed one he wrote himself about the
time he badly injured his knee and had to lie in hospital when
he should have been playing football.

I'm Not Conceited

by J.E.C.F.

Oh dear no, I'm not conceited
But my way's always best
Susannah now I call conceited
She sets herself above the rest.

I don't consider I'm conceited
You always find my reasons true,
And if you don't—why then the fault is
Clearly not in me, but you.

Others too may have opinions!
Yes, but they should be like mine.
They so often choose the wrong ones.
I'm right ten times out of nine!

Chosen by **Charles Farncombe**, Musical Director of the Malcolm Sargent
Festival Choir

‘A stay with Grandpa and Grandma was always exciting. The humdrum respectability of a council housing estate was exchanged for a week of real adventure.

They lived in one room in a tenement house in Cable Street off the Minories. A tap and stone sink on the half landing was the only water supply and the loo was at the bottom of the "airey". At night they would pull a curtain across one end of the room where I slept on two chairs tied together, to shade me from the light of the inverted gas mantle.

Life was colourful—for Grandpa had a coffee stall on Tower Hill. As now, there was a sword swallower, a fire eater and a man who could release himself from any number of chains, to amuse passers by. But most fascinating were Grandpa's "regulars". The old man who looked so poor, and who would empty out his pockets of half pennies and farthings on to the counter for Grandpa to count out. The detectives in workers clothes (you always knew them by their unspoiled hands!) and "Old Dogger", the lighterman who would give me a free ride on a barge which he happened to be ferrying across to Vaisey's Wharf.

Grandpa served them with large mugs of tea or "Camp" coffee together with thick sandwiches of cheese, bacon or brawn or a slice of Tottenham Cake from a wire tray.

On Sunday mornings we arose at 6.30 and swam in Hackney Baths. The rest of the day we walked around the City exploring unknown treasures—the boy in Panyer Alley—the golden boy opposite Bart's. We always went to a service at St Magnus the Martyr by London Bridge, where the church was decorated with fish for Harvest Festival—the plaice around the Altar Cross was as tall as me! When we were the only congregation, the beadle would come down and whisper to Grandpa: "The Rector presents his compliments, and would you wish to hear a sermon?" My hopes were always dashed by Grandpa's reply. Back to Cable Street for tea of winkles or crumpets to finish the day.

As you entered the front door, amid dingy brown paint and worn lino, you were confronted by two framed illustrations on the wall. The one was Patti singing in *Lucia di Lammermuir* at Covent Garden. Grandpa had been an army bandsman and boasted that he had played 1st bassoon for some of her performances. The other was an illustrated poem from "Chatterbox", showing a boy in an Eton Collar and suit, bowler hat with his nose high in the air which read: "I'm not conceited".’

Home-Sickness

by Charlotte Brontë

Of College I am tired; I wish to be at home,
Far from the pompous tutor's voice, and the hated
    school-boy's groan.

I wish that I had freedom to walk about at will;
That I no more was troubled by my Greek and slate
    and quill.

I wish to see my kitten, to hear my ape rejoice,
To listen to my nightingale's or parrot's lovely voice.

And England does not suit me: it's cold and full of
    snow;
So different from black Africa's warm, sunny, genial
    glow.

I'm shivering in the day-time, and shivering all the
    night:
I'm called poor, startled, withered wretch, and miserable
    wight!

And oh! I miss my brother, I miss his gentle smile
Which used so many long dark hours of sorrow to
    beguile.

I miss my dearest mother; I now no longer find
Aught half so mild as she was,—so careful and so kind.

Oh, I have not my father's, my noble father's arms
To guard me from all wickedness, and keep me safe
    from harms.

I hear his voice no longer; I see no more his eye
Smile on me in my misery: to whom now shall I fly?

Chosen by **Rabbi Julia Neuberger**

❮It rang bells of memories when away from home on holiday
projects.❯

From Northampton Asylum

by John Clare

I am, but what I am who cares or knows?
My friends forsake me like a memory lost.
I am the self-consumer of my woes,
And yet I am—I live. Though I am tossed

Into a nothingness of scorn and noise,
Into a living sea of waking dreams.
Where there is neither sense of life nor joys
But the huge shipwreck of my esteem,
And all that's dear. Even those I loved the best
Are strange. Nay, they are stranger than the rest.

I long for scenes where man has never trod
For scenes where woman never smiled nor wept,
There to remain with my creator—God
And sleep as I in childhood sweetly slept
Full of high thoughts unborn. So let me lie
The grass beneath; above the vaulted sky.

Chosen by **Dorothy Tutin** CBE, actress

❮I was about fourteen when I found this poem, and had a
deeply morbid imagination. I used to think a lot about infinity
and timelessness, and why we are here, and this poem both
consoled and frightened me.❯

A Red, Red Rose

by Robert Burns

My love is like a red, red rose
    That's newly sprung in June:
My love is like the melody
    That's sweetly played in tune.

As fair art thou, my bonnie lass,
    So deep in love am I:
And I will love thee still, my dear,
    Till a' the seas gang dry.

Till a' the seas gang dry, my dear,
    And the rocks melt wi' the sun:
And I will love thee still, my dear,
    While the sands o' life shall run.

And fare thee weel, my only love,
  And fare thee weel a while!
And I will come again, my love,
  Thou' it were ten thousand mile.

Chosen by **Bobby Charlton** CBE, former England footballer with over 100 caps

❛This is my favourite poem.❜

Abou Ben Adhem

by Leigh Hunt

Abou Ben Adhem (may his tribe increase!)
Awoke one night from a deep dream of peace,
And saw, within the moonlight in his room,
Making it rich, and like a lily in bloom,
An angel writing in a book of gold:—
Exceeding peace had made Ben Adhem bold,
And to the presence in the room he said,
    'What writest thou?'—The vision raised its head,
And with a look made of all sweet accord,
Answered, 'The names of those who love the Lord.'
'And is mine one?' said Abou. 'Nay, not so,'
Replied the angel. Abou spoke more low,
But cheerly still; and said, 'I pray thee, then,
Write me as one that loves his fellow men.'
    The angel wrote, and vanished. The next night
It came again with a great wakening light,
And showed the names whom love of God had blest,
And lo! Ben Adhem's name led all the rest.

Chosen by **Sir Yehudi Menuhin**, violinist and conductor

Lochinvar

by Sir Walter Scott

O, young Lochinvar is come out of the west,
Through all the wide Border his steed was the best;
And save his good broadsword he weapons had none,
He rode all unarmed, and he rode all alone.
So faithful in love, and so dauntless in war,
There never was knight like the young Lochinvar.

He stayed not for brake, and he stopped not for stone,
He swam the Eske river where ford there was none;
But ere he alighted at Netherby gate,
The bride had consented, the gallant came late:
For a laggard in love, and a dastard in war,
Was to wed the fair Ellen of brave Lochinvar.

So boldly he entered the Netherby Hall,
Among bride's men, and kinsmen, and brothers, and all:
Then spoke the bride's father, his hand on his sword,
(For the poor craven bridegroom said never a word,)
'O come ye in peace here, or come ye in war,
Or to dance at our bridal, young Lord Lochinvar?'

'I long wooed your daughter, my suit you denied;—
Love swells like the Solway, but ebbs like its tide—
And now am I come, with this lost love of mine,
To lead but one measure, drink one cup of wine.
There are maidens in Scotland more lovely by far,
That would gladly be bride to the young Lochinvar.'

The bride kissed the goblet: the knight took it up,
He quaffed off the wine, and he threw down the cup.
She looked down to blush, and she looked up to sigh,
With a smile on her lips, and a tear in her eye.
He took her soft hand, ere her mother could bar,—
'Now tread we a measure!' said young Lochinvar.

So stately his form, and so lovely her face,
That never a hall such a galliard did grace;
While her mother did fret, and her father did fume,
And the bridegroom stood dangling his bonnet and
plume;
And the bride-maidens whispered, ' 'Twere better by
far,
To have matched our fair cousin with young Lochinvar.'

One touch to her hand, and one word in her ear,
When they reached the hall-door, and the charger stood
near;
So light to the croupe the fair lady he swung,
So light to the saddle before her he sprung!
'She is won! we are gone, over bank, bush, and scaur;
They'll have fleet steeds that follow,' quoth young
Lochinvar.

There was mounting 'mong Græmes of the Netherby
clan;
Forsters, Fenwicks, and Musgraves, they rode and they
ran:
There was racing and chasing on Cannonbie Lee,
But the lost bride of Netherby ne'er did they see.
So daring in love, and so dauntless in war,
Have ye e'er heard of gallant like young Lochinvar?

Chosen by **Eric Anderson**, Head Master of Eton

❛Both the rhythm and the romantic historical theme of
Lochinvar appealed to me when I was made to learn the
poem at school as a young boy. There are Border farmers
among my forebears and that no doubt also disposed me in
its favour.❜

The Night-Piece, to Julia

by Robert Herrick

Her Eyes the Glow-worme lend thee,
The Shooting Starres attend thee;
    And the Elves also,
    Whose little eyes flow,
Like the sparks of fire, befriend thee.

No *Will-o'-th'Wispe* mis-light thee;
Nor Snake, or Slow-worme bite thee:
    But on, on thy way
    Not making a stay,
Since Ghost ther's none to affright thee.

Let not the darke thee cumber;
What though the Moon do's slumber?
    The Starres of the night
    Will lend thee their light,
Like Tapers cleare without number.

Then *Julia* let me wooe thee,
Thus, thus to come unto me:
    And when I shall meet
    Thy silv'ry feet,
My soule Ile poure into thee.

Chosen by **Jilly Cooper**, author

❛My mother used to read me poetry as a child and as I was very frightened of the dark, she read me Herrick's *Night-Piece*. It helped me a lot and comforted me a great deal and I've always thought it was an incredibly beautiful poem.❜

Lord Lundy,

Who was too Freely Moved to Tears, and thereby ruined his Political Career

by Hilaire Belloc

Lord Lundy from his earliest years
Was far too freely moved to Tears.
For instance if his Mother said,
'Lundy! It's time to go to Bed!'
He bellowed like a Little Turk.
Or if his father Lord Dunquerque
Said 'Hi!' in a Commanding Tone,
'Hi, Lundy! Leave the Cat alone!'
Lord Lundy, letting go its tail,
Would raise so terrible a wail
As moved His Grandpapa the Duke
To utter the severe rebuke:
'When I, Sir! was a little Boy,
An Animal was not a Toy!'
His father's Elder Sister, who
Was married to a Parvenoo,
Confided to Her Husband, 'Drat!
The Miserable, Peevish Brat!
Why don't they drown the Little Beast?'
Suggestions which, to say the least,
Are not what we expect to hear
From Daughters of an English Peer.
His grandmamma, His Mother's Mother,
Who had some dignity or other,
The Garter, or no matter what,
I can't remember all the Lot!
Said 'Oh! that I were Brisk and Spry
To give him that for which to cry!'
(An empty wish, alas! for she
Was Blind and nearly ninety-three).

The Dear old Butler thought—but there!
I really neither know nor care
For what the Dear Old Butler thought!
In my opinion, Butlers ought
To know their place, and not to play
The Old Retainer night and day
I'm getting tired and so are you,
Let's cut the Poem into two!

*   *   *   *   *

Lord Lundy

(Second Canto)

It happened to Lord Lundy then,
As happens to so many men:
Towards the age of twenty-six,
They shoved him into politics;
In which profession he commanded
The income that his rank demanded
In turn as Secretary for
India, the Colonies, and War.
But very soon his friends began
To doubt if he were quite the man:
Thus, if a member rose to say
(As members do from day to day),
'Arising out of that reply . . . !'
Lord Lundy would begin to cry.
A Hint at harmless little jobs
Would shake him with convulsive sobs.

While as for Revelations, these
Would simply bring him to his knees,
And leave him whimpering like a child.
It drove his Colleagues raving wild!
They let him sink from Post to Post,
From fifteen hundred at the most
To eight, and barely six—and then
To be Curator of Big Ben! . . .
And finally there came a Threat
To oust him from the Cabinet!

The Duke—his aged grand-sire—bore
The shame till he could bear no more.
He rallied his declining powers,
Summoned the youth to Brackley Towers,
And bitterly addressed him thus—
'Sir! you have disappointed us!
We had intended you to be
The next Prime Minister but three:
The stocks were sold; the Press was squared:
The Middle Class was quite prepared.
But as it is! . . . My language fails!
Go out and govern New South Wales!'

      *   *   *   *   *

The Aged Patriot groaned and died:
And gracious! how Lord Lundy cried!

Chosen by **Sir Peter Ustinov**, actor, dramatist and wit

❛I love it for its wonderful lines: "My language fails! Go out and govern New South Wales!"❜

from King John's Christmas

by A.A. Milne

King John was not a good man—
   He had his little ways.
And sometimes no one spoke to him
   For days and days and days.
And men who came across him,
   When walking in the town,
Gave him a supercilious stare,
Or passed with noses in the air—
And bad King John stood dumbly there,
   Blushing beneath his crown.

King John was not a good man,
   And no good friends had he.
He stayed in every afternoon . . .
   But no one came to tea.
And, round about December,
   The cards upon his shelf
Which wished him lots of Christmas cheer,
And fortune in the coming year,
Were never from his near and dear.
   But only from himself.

King John was not a good man,
   Yet had his hopes and fears.
They'd given him no present now
   For years and years and years.
But every year at Christmas,
   While minstrels stood about,
Collecting tribute from the young
For all the songs they might have sung,
He stole away upstairs and hung
   A hopeful stocking out.

King John was not a good man,
  He lived his life aloof;
Alone he thought a message out
  While climbing up the roof.
He wrote it down and propped it
  Against the chimney stack:
'TO ALL AND SUNDRY—NEAR AND FAR—
F. CHRISTMAS IN PARTICULAR.'
And signed it not 'Johannes R.'
  But very humbly, 'JACK.'

'I want some crackers,
  And I want some candy;
I think a box of chocolates
  Would come in handy;
I don't mind oranges,
  I do like nuts!
And I SHOULD like a pocket-knife
  That really cuts.
And, oh! Father Christmas, if you love me at all,
Bring me a big, red india-rubber ball!'

King John was not a good man—
  Next morning when the sun
Rose up to tell a waiting world
  That Christmas had begun,
And people seized their stockings,
  And opened them with glee,
And crackers, toys and games appeared,
And lips with sticky sweets were smeared,
King John said grimly: 'As I feared,
  Nothing again for me!'

'I did want crackers,
    And I did want candy;
I know a box of chocolates
    Would come in handy;
I do love oranges,
    I did want nuts.
I haven't got a pocket-knife—
    Not one that cuts.
And, oh! if Father Christmas had loved me at all,
He would have brought a big, red india-rubber ball!'

King John stood by the window,
    And frowned to see below
The happy bands of boys and girls
    All playing in the snow.
A while he stood there watching,
    And envying them all . . .
When through the window big and red
There hurtled by his royal head,
And bounced and fell upon the bed,
    An india-rubber ball!

AND OH, FATHER CHRISTMAS,
    MY BLESSINGS ON YOU FALL
        FOR BRINGING HIM
        A BIG, RED,
        INDIA-RUBBER
        BALL!

Chosen by the **Rt Hon Paddy Ashdown** MP, Leader of the Liberal Democrat Party

Henry VIII

by Eleanor and Herbert Farjeon

Bluff King Hal was full of beans;
He married half a dozen queens;
For three called Kate they cried the banns,
And one called Jane, and a couple of Annes.

The first he asked to share his reign
Was Kate of Aragon, straight from Spain—
But when his love for her was spent,
He got a divorce, and out she went.

Anne Boleyn was his second wife;
He swore to cherish her all his life—
But seeing a third he wished instead,
He chopped off poor Anne Boleyn's head.

He married the next afternoon
Jane Seymour, which was rather soon—
But after one year as his bride
She crept into her bed and died.

Anne of Cleves was Number Four;
Her portrait thrilled him to the core—
But when he met her face to face
Another royal divorce took place.

Catherine Howard, Number Five,
Billed and cooed to keep alive—
But one day Henry felt depressed;
The executioner did the rest.

Sixth and last came Catherine Parr,
Sixth and last and luckiest far—
For this time it was Henry who
Hopped the twig, and a good job too.

Chosen by **Katharine Whitehorn**, columnist for *The Observer*

❬I remember much enjoying *Henry VIII*, and indeed this is the only way I can remember his queens even now.❭

Part 3
AWAY DOWN THE VALLEY, AWAY DOWN THE HILL
Poems About Travelling

Adlestrop
by Edward Thomas

Yes, I remember Adlestrop—
The name, because one afternoon
Of heat the express-train drew up there
Unwontedly. It was late June.

The steam hissed. Someone cleared his throat.
No one left and no one came
On the bare platform. What I saw
Was Adlestrop—only the name.

And willows, willow-herb, and grass,
And meadowsweet, and haycocks dry,
No whit less still and lonely fair
Than the high cloudlets in the sky.

And for that minute a blackbird sang
Close by, and round him, mistier,
Farther and farther, all the birds
Of Oxfordshire and Gloucestershire.

Chosen by **Jane Asher**, actress, writer and famous for her wonderful cakes

❛It is hard to say why this particular poem moves me so much—if I could put into words exactly what it means to me I'd be a poet myself! I've loved it since my school days.❜

from The Son of God Goes Forth

by Bishop R. Heber

The son of God goes forth to war,
   A kingly crown to gain;
His blood-red banner streams afar:
   Who follows in his train?

Who best can drink his cup of woe,
   Triumphant over pain,
Who patient bears his cross below,
   He follows in his train.

A noble army, men and boys,
   The matron and the maid,
Around the Saviour's throne rejoice
   In robes of light arrayed.

They climbed the steep ascent of heaven
   Through peril, toil, and pain:
O God, to us may grace be given
   To follow in their train.

Chosen by **Sir David Willcocks**, Musical Director of the Bach Choir

❛Memories of happy years as a boy in the choir of Westminster
Abbey. I liked to picture the men and boys of the choir,
accompanied by the Choir School matron and the maid,
arrayed in robes of white, having climbed the steep ascent
of heaven in a train resembling the Cornish Riviera on which I
used to travel home for holidays.❜

I Had a Baby Austin

Anon

I had a baby Austin
I found it most exhaustin'
I could get in my feet
And a part of my seat
But the rest of me had to be forced in

Chosen by **Sir Andrew Hugh Smith**, Chairman of the London Stock Exchange

❛It is the only poem I can remember, and was taught to me with great difficulty by my father's elderly nanny, aged about eighty, when I was four.❜

To a Car

by Dame Barbara Cartland

Your headlamps like two golden moons
    Shine on the silver way,
The wind is singing you faery tunes,
    Drive on till you find the day.
Adventures are there in the dusky trees
    There where the blue mists lie,
Adventures crooned by the murmuring breeze
    To the flowers—their lullaby.
Have you forgotten Peter Pan,
    Tink and the pirate crew,
The song of the jungle Mowgli sang,
    The cry the wolf-pack knew?
Down in the cities the flaring lights
    Of brothel, bar and street
Are filled with gaudy 'fly-by-nights',
    Those vultures seeking meat.
Here, with the flickering lights away,
    Away in the night-hid town,
You will, perhaps hear an Angel say:
    'Why the stars have fallen down.'
Over the hills and far away
    Your headlamps like golden moons
Driven on till the break of day,
    With the wind-sung faery tunes.

Chosen by **Dame Barbara Cartland** DBE DStJ, romantic novelist

❝It was written by me in 1920 about a car, which was still quite a novelty at that time.❞

Sea Fever

by John Masefield

I must down to the seas again, to the lonely sea and
    the sky,
And all I ask is a tall ship and a star to steer her by,
And the wheel's kick and the wind's song and the white
    sails shaking,
And a grey mist on the sea's face and a grey dawn
    breaking.

I must down to the seas again, for the call of the
    running tide
Is a wild call and a clear call that may not be denied;
And all I ask is a windy day with the white clouds
    flying,
And the flung spray and the blown spume, and the sea-
    gulls crying.

I must down to the seas again, to the vagrant gypsy life,
To the gull's way and the whale's way where the wind's
    like a whetted knife;
And all I ask is a merry yarn from a laughing fellow-
    rover,
And quiet sleep and a sweet dream when the long
    trick's over.

Chosen by **The Rt Hon Norman Lamont** MP, ex-Chancellor of the Exchequer

The Old Ships

by James Elroy Flecker

I have seen old ships sail like swans asleep
Beyond the village which men still call Tyre,
With leaden age o'ercargoed, dipping deep
For Famagusta and the hidden sun
That rings black Cyprus with a lake of fire;
And all those ships were certainly so old
Who knows how oft with squat and noisy gun,
Questing brown slaves or Syrian oranges,
The pirates Genoese
Hell-raked them till they rolled
Blood, water, fruit and corpses up the hold.
But now through friendly seas they softly run,
Painted the mid-sea blue or, shore-sea green,
Still patterned with the vine and grapes in gold.

But I have seen,
Pointing her shapely shadows from the dawn
And image tumbled on a rose-swept bay,
A drowsy ship of some yet older day;
And, wonder's breath indrawn,
Thought I—who knows—who knows—but in that same
(Fished up beyond Aeaea, patched up new
—Stern painted brighter blue—)
That talkative, bald-headed seaman came
(Twelve patient comrades sweating at the oar)
From Troy's doom-crimson shore,
And with great lies about his wooden horse
Set the crew laughing, and forgot his course.

It was so old a ship—who knows, who knows?
—And yet so beautiful, I watched in vain
To see the mast burst open with a rose,
And the whole deck put on its leaves again.

‘When I was young I didn't understand half the allusions of this gloriously romantic poem, but I loved the lush words of it, the exotic suggestions, the music and the general sense of golden excitement far away. Just the word "ship" thrills me always.’

Becalmed

by John Paul Ross

Pass round the water carefully,
A sip is enough each, mate
Bring out the harp,
We can listen to its tuneless tollings,
Least another hour,
Occupy your tortured minds,
But do not fall asleep,
Fatigue is our most dreadful enemy,
For if we fall asleep,
Who knows?

We might not wake.
Huh, a joke
Our sorry half starved souls.
Would be little addition to
Jones locker,
Wait, a thunder storm's arising,
Heaven be praised.

Chosen by **Jonathan Ross**, television personality and chat show host

❛I remember few poems from my youth, but there is one that sticks in my mind. It was written by my eldest brother, Paul, when he was about eleven years old. He entered the Ninth *Daily Mirror* Children's Literary Competition with it, and it was selected to be published in the book that always followed the competition. He received a prize of £10 for it, with which he treated my other brothers, one sister and myself to presents of toys and sweets.❜

Cargoes

by John Masefield

Quinquireme of Nineveh from distant Ophir
Rowing home to haven in sunny Palestine,
With a cargo of ivory,
And apes and peacocks,
Sandalwood, cedarwood, and sweet white wine.

Stately Spanish galleon coming from the Isthmus,
Dipping through the Tropics by the palm-green shores,
With a cargo of diamonds,
Emeralds, amethysts,
Topazes, and cinnamon, and gold moidores.

Dirty British coaster with a salt-caked smoke stack
Butting through the Channel in the mad March days,
With a cargo of Tyne coal,
Road-rail, pig-lead,
Firewood, iron-ware, and cheap tin trays.

Chosen by **Mary Whitehouse**, President of the National Viewers and Listeners Association and **Miriam Stoppard**, doctor, writer and broadcaster

❝I said it over and over again in my childhood, and later. It transported me, especially the second verse, and even the third verse had a magic about it.❞
Mary Whitehouse

❝It was the mention of Tyne coal in the last verse; I was born on Tyneside—it seemed to be all soot and slag heaps, and then there we were—in a poem—rhythm and romance. Racey.❞
Miriam Stoppard

Big Steamers

by Rudyard Kipling

'Oh, where are you going to, all you Big Steamers,
    With England's own coal, up and down the salt
        seas?'
'We are going to fetch you your bread and your butter,
    Your beef, pork, and mutton, eggs, apples, and
        cheese.'

'And where will you fetch it from, all you Big Steamers,
    And where shall I write you when you are away?'
'We fetch it from Melbourne, Quebec, and
        Vancouver—
    Address us at Hobart, Hong Kong, and Bombay.'

'But if anything happened to all you Big Steamers,
     And suppose you were wrecked up and down the
          salt sea?'
'Then you'd have no coffee or bacon for breakfast,
     And you'd have no muffins or toast for your tea.'

'Then I'll pray for fine weather for all you Big Steamers,
     For little blue billows and breezes so soft.'
'Oh, billows and breezes don't bother Big Steamers,
     for we're iron below and steel-rigging aloft.'

'Then I'll build a new lighthouse for all you Big
          Steamers,
     With plenty wise pilots to pilot you through.'
'Oh, the Channel's as bright as a ball-room already,
     And pilots are thicker than pilchards at Looe.'

'Then what can I do for you, all you Big Steamers,
     Oh, what can I do for your comfort and good?'
'Send out your big warships to watch your big waters,
     That no one may stop us from bringing your food.

'For the bread that you eat and the biscuits you nibble,
     The sweets that you suck and the joints that you carve,
They are brought to you daily by all us Big Steamers—
     And if any one hinders our coming you'll starve!'

Where Go the Boats?

by Robert Louis Stevenson

Dark brown is the river,
   Golden is the sand.
It flows along for ever,
   With trees on either hand.

Green leaves a-floating,
   Castles of the foam,
Boats of mine a-boating—
   Where will all come home?

On goes the river
   And out past the mill,
Away down the valley,
   Away down the hill.

Away down the river,
  A hundred miles or more,
Other little children
  Shall bring my boats ashore.

Chosen by **Ludovic Kennedy**, writer and broadcaster

from How They Brought the Good News from Ghent to Aix

by Robert Browning

I sprang to the stirrup, and Joris, and he;
I galloped, Dirck galloped, we galloped all three;
'Good speed!' cried the watch, as the gate-bolts undrew;
'Speed!' echoed the wall to us galloping through;
Behind shut the postern, the lights sank to rest,
And into the midnight we galloped abreast.

Not a word to each other; we kept the great pace
Neck by neck, stride by stride, never changing our
    place;
I turned in my saddle and made its girths tight,
Then shortened each stirrup, and set the pique right,
Rebuckled the cheek-strap, chained slacker the bit,
Nor galloped less steadily Roland a whit.

'Twas moonset at starting; but while we drew near
Lokern, the cocks crew and twilight dawned clear;
At Boom, a great yellow star came out to see;
At Düffield, 'twas morning as plain as could be;
And from Mecheln church-steeple we heard the half-
    chime,
So Joris broke silence with, 'Yet there is time!'

At Aerschot, up leaped of a sudden the sun,
And against him the cattle stood black every one,
To stare thro' the mist at us galloping past,
And I saw my stout galloper Roland at last,
With resolute shoulders, each butting away
The haze, as some bluff river headland its spray.

And his low head and crest, just one sharp ear bent
    back
For my voice, and the other pricked out on his track;
And one eye's black intelligence, ever that glance
O'er its white edge at me, his own master, askance!
And the thick heavy spume-flakes which aye and anon
His fierce lips shook upwards in galloping on.

By Hasselt, Dirck groaned; and cried Joris, 'Stay spur!
'Your Roos galloped bravely, the fault's not in her,
'We'll remember at Aix'—for one heard the quick
    wheeze
Of her chest, saw the stretched neck and staggering
    knees,
And sunk tail, and horrible heave of the flank,
As down on her haunches she shuddered and sank.

So we were left galloping, Joris and I,
Past Looz and past Tongres, no cloud in the sky;
The broad sun above laughed a pitiless laugh,
'Neath our feet broke the brittle bright stubble like
    chaff;
Till over by Dalhem a dome-spire sprang white,
And 'Gallop,' gasped Joris, 'for Aix is in sight!'

'How they'll greet us!'—and all in a moment his roan
Rolled neck and croup over, lay dead as a stone;
And there was my Roland to bear the whole weight
Of the news which alone could save Aix from her fate,
With his nostrils like pits full of blood to the brim,
And with circles of red for his eye-sockets' rim.

Then I cast loose my buffcoat, each holster let fall,
Shook off both my jack-boots, let go belt and all,
Stood up in the stirrup, leaned, patted his ear,
Called my Roland his pet-name, my horse without peer;
Clapped my hands, laughed and sang, any noise, bad or
        good,
Till at length into Aix Roland galloped and stood.

And all I remember is, friends flocking round
As I sate with his head 'twixt my knees on the ground,
And no voice but was praising this Roland of mine,
As I poured down his throat our last measure of wine,
Which (the burgesses voted by common consent)
Was no more than his due who brought good news
        from Ghent.

The Table and the Chair

by Edward Lear

Said the Table to the Chair,
'You can hardly be aware,
'How I suffer from the heat,
'And from chilblains on my feet!
'If we took a little walk,
'We might have a little talk!
'Pray let us take the air!'
Said the Table to the Chair.

Said the Chair unto the Table,
'Now you *know* we are not able!
'How foolishly you talk,
'When you know we *cannot* walk!'
Said the Table, with a sigh,
'It can do no harm to try,
'I've as many legs as you,
'Why can't we walk on two?'

So they both went slowly down,
And walked about the town
With a cheerful bumpy sound,
As they toddled round and round.
And everybody cried,
As they hastened to their side,
'See! the Table and the Chair
'Have come out to take the air!'

But in going down an alley,
To a castle in a valley,
They completely lost their way,
And wandered all the day,
Till, to see them safely back,
They paid a Ducky-quack,
And a Beetle, and a Mouse,
Who took them to their house.

Then they whispered to each other,
'O delightful little brother!
'What a lovely walk we've taken!
'Let us dine on Beans and Bacon!'
So the Ducky, and the leetle
Browny-Mousy and the Beetle
Dined, and danced upon their heads
Till they toddled to their beds.

Chosen by **George Melly**, jazz musician, writer and critic

❛An elderly relation in Liverpool loved to read me Lear and
Beatrix Potter when I was a creature of pure wonder (ie 5–8
years old). I've chosen this poem (it could have been any)
because it is shorter than most, less well known, and has that
marvellous mixture of melancholy and humour common to all.❜

Part 4

I HAVE FOUGHT SUCH A FIGHT
Poems of War and Peace

The Roman Centurion's Song
by Rudyard Kipling

Legate, I had the news last night—my cohort ordered
    home
By ship to Portus Itius and thence by road to Rome.
I've marched the companies aboard, the arms are stowed
    below:
Now let another take my sword. Command me not to
    go!

I've served in Britain forty years, from Vectis to the
    Wall.
I have none other home than this, nor any life at all.
Last night I did not understand, but, now the hour
    draws near
That calls me to my native land, I feel that land is
    here.

Here where men say my name was made, here where
    my work was done;
Here where my dearest dead are laid—my wife—my
    wife and son;
Here where time, custom, grief and toil, age, memory,
    service, love,
Have rooted me in British soil. Ah, how can I remove?

For me this land, that sea, these airs, those folk and
    fields suffice.
What purple Southern pomp can match our changeful
    Northern skies,
Black with December snows unshed or pearled with
    August haze—
The clanging arch of steel-grey March, or June's long-
    lighted days?

You'll follow widening Rhodanus till vine and olive
    lean
Aslant before the sunny breeze that sweeps Nemausus
    clean
To Arelate's triple gate; but let me linger on,
Here where our stiff-necked British oaks confront
    Euroclydon!

You'll take the old Aurelian Road through shore-
    descending pines
Where, blue as any peacock's neck, the Tyrrhene Ocean
    shines.
You'll go where laurel crowns are won, but—will you
    e'er forget
The scent of hawthorn in the sun, or bracken in the
    wet?

Let me work here for Britain's sake—at any task you
    will—
A marsh to drain, a road to make or native troops to
    drill.
Some Western camp (I know the Pict) or granite Border
    keep,
Mid seas of heather derelict, where our old messmates
    sleep.

Legate, I come to you in tears—My cohort ordered
    home!
I've served in Britain forty years. What should I do in
    Rome?
Here is my heart, my soul, my mind—the only life I
    know.
I cannot leave it all behind. Command me not to go!

Chosen by **Patrick Leigh Fermor**, author and travel writer

❛I learnt this poem when I was seven, when *Puck of Pook's
Hill* and *Rewards and Fairies* [collections of stories based on
English history, by Rudyard Kipling] were being read aloud to
my sister and me. It has haunted and enchanted me ever
since.❜

The Destruction of Sennacherib

by Lord Byron

The Assyrian came down like the wolf on the fold,
And his cohorts were gleaming in purple and gold;
And the sheen of his spears was like stars on the sea
When the blue wave rolls nightly on deep Galilee.

Like the leaves of the forest when Summer is green,
That host with their banners at sunset were seen:
Like the leaves of the forest when Autumn hath blown,
That lost on the morrow lay wither'd and strown.

For the Angel of Death spread his wings on the blast,
And breathed in the face of the foe as he pass'd;
And the eyes of the sleepers wax'd deadly and chill,
And their hearts but once heaved, and for ever grew
    still!

And there lay the steed with his nostril all wide,
But through it there roll'd not the breath of his pride;
And the foam of his gasping lay white on the turf,
And cold as the spray of the rock-beating surf.

And there lay the rider distorted and pale,
With the dew on his brow, and the rust on his mail;
And the tents were all silent, the banners alone,
The lances unlifted, the trumpet unblown.

And the widows of Ashur are loud in their wail,
And the idols are broke in the temple of Baal;
And the might of the Gentile, unsmote by the sword,
Hath melted like snow in the glance of the Lord!

Chosen by **Frederic Raphael**, playwright, novelist and biographer

❛I like this poem for all sorts of reasons. It is easy to remember;
it contains more lines beginning with "And" than one can well
support; it is euphonious and vivid and gives you the feeling
that you too could write verses; its sentiments are entirely moral,
although it is, I daresay, *slightly* despicable to rejoice in the
Assyrians being defeated more by what sounds like an
epidemic than a fair fight. It is gorgeous, facile stuff—but try
to write anything a quarter as bracing!❜

Drake's Drum

by Sir Henry Newbolt

Drake he's in his hammock an' a thousand mile away,
    (Capten, art tha sleepin' there below?),
Slung atween the round shot in Nombre Dios Bay,
    An' dreamin' arl the time o' Plymouth Hoe.
Yarnder lumes the Island, yarnder lie the ships,
    Wi' sailor lads a dancin' heel-an'-toe,
An' the shore-lights flashin', an' the night-tide dashin',
    He sees et arl so plainly as he saw et long ago.

Drake he was a Devon man, an' rüled the Devon seas,
    (Capten, art tha sleepin' there below?),
Rovin' tho' his death fell, he went wi' heart at ease,
    An' dreamin' arl the time o' Plymouth Hoe.
'Take my drum to England, hang et by the shore,
    Strike et when your powder's runnin' low;
If the Dons sight Devon, I'll quit the port o' Heaven,
    An' drum them up the Channel as we drummed
        them long ago.'

Drake he's in his hammock till the great Armadas come,
    (Capten, art tha sleepin' there below?),
Slung atween the round shot, listenin' for the drum,
    An' dreamin' arl the time o' Plymouth Hoe.
Call him on the deep sea, call him up the Sound,
    Call him when ye sail to meet the foe;
Where the old trades' plyin' an' the old flag flyin'
    They shall find him ware an' wakin', as they found
        him long ago!

Chosen by **Robert Powell**, actor

❲The first poem I ever learnt and performed in front of an audience—at my primary school, aged seven years!❳

from The Revenge

A Ballad of the Fleet

by Alfred, Lord Tennyson

At Flores in the Azores Sir Richard Grenville lay,
And a pinnace, like a fluttered bird, came flying from
    far away:
'Spanish ships of war at sea! we have sighted fifty-
    three!'
Then sware Lord Thomas Howard: ' 'Fore God I am no
    coward;
But I cannot meet them here, for my ships are out of gear,
And the half my men are sick. I must fly, but follow quick.
We are six ships of the line; can we fight with fifty-three?'

Then spake Sir Richard Grenville: 'I know you are no
    coward;
You fly them for a moment to fight with them again.
But I've ninety men and more that are lying sick ashore.
I should count myself the coward if I left them, my
    Lord Howard,
To these Inquisition dogs and the devildoms of Spain.'

So Lord Howard past away with five ships of war that
    day,
Till he melted like a cloud in the silent summer heaven;
But Sir Richard bore in hand all his sick men from the
    land
Very carefully and slow,
Men of Bideford in Devon,
And we laid them on the ballast down below;
For we brought them all aboard,
And they blest him in their pain, that they were not
    left to Spain,
To the thumbscrew and the stake, for the glory of the
    Lord.

He had only a hundred seamen to work the ship and
to fight,
And he sailed away from Flores till the Spaniard came
in sight,
With his huge sea-castles heaving upon the weather bow.
'Shall we fight or shall we fly?
Good Sir Richard, tell us now,
For to fight is but to die!
There'll be little of us left by the time this sun be set.'
And Sir Richard said again: 'We be all good English men.
Let us bang these dogs of Seville, the children of the devil,
For I never turned my back upon Don or devil yet.'

Sir Richard spoke and he laughed, and we roared a
hurrah, and so
The little *Revenge* ran on sheer into the heart of the foe,
With her hundred fighters on deck, and her ninety sick
below;
For half of their fleet to the right and half to the left
were seen,
And the little *Revenge* ran on through the long sea-
lane between.

And the sun went down, and the stars came out far
over the summer sea,
But never a moment ceased the fight of the one and
the fifty-three.
Ship after ship, the whole night long, their high-built
galleons came,
Ship after ship, the whole night long, with her battle-
thunder and flame;
Ship after ship, the whole night long, drew back with
her dead and her shame.
For some were sunk and many were shattered, and so
could fight us no more—
God of battles, was ever a battle like this in the world
before?

For he said 'Fight on! fight on!'
Though his vessel was all but a wreck;
And it chanced that, when half of the short summer
    night was gone,
With a grisly wound to be dressed he had left the deck,
But a bullet struck him that was dressing it suddenly
    dead,
And himself he was wounded again in the side and the
    head,
And he said 'Fight on! fight on!'

And the night went down, and the sun smiled out far
    over the summer sea,
And the Spanish fleet with broken sides lay round us
    all in a ring;
But they dared not touch us again, for they feared that
    we still could sting,
So they watched what the end would be.
And we had not fought them in vain,
But in perilous plight were we,
Seeing forty of our poor hundred were slain,
And half of the rest of us maimed for life
In the crash of the cannonades and the desperate strife;
And the sick men down in the hold were most of them
    stark and cold,
And the pikes were all broken or bent, and the powder
    was all of it spent;
And the masts and the rigging were lying over the side;
But Sir Richard cried in his English pride,
'We have fought such a fight for a day and a night
As may never be fought again!
We have won great glory, my men!
And a day less or more
At sea or ashore,
We die—does it matter when?

Sink me the ship, Master Gunner—sink her, split her
    in twain!
Fall into the hands of God, not into the hands of
    Spain!'
And the gunner said 'Ay, ay,' but the seamen made
    reply:
'We have children, we have wives,
And the Lord hath spared our lives.
We will make the Spaniard promise, if we yield, to let
    us go;
We shall live to fight again and to strike another blow.'
And the lion there lay dying, and they yielded to the
    foe.

And the stately Spanish men to their flagship bore him
    then,
Where they laid him by the mast, old Sir Richard
    caught at last,
And they praised him to his face with their courtly
    foreign grace;
But he rose upon their decks, and he cried:
'I have fought for Queen and Faith like a valiant man
    and true;
I have only done my duty as a man is bound to do:
With a joyful spirit I Sir Richard Grenville die!'
And he fell upon their decks, and he died.

Chosen by **Bruce Kent**, campaigner for disarmament and former Chairman
of CND (Campaign for Nuclear Disarmament)

❛Whenever my father was feeling patriotic and British he would
recite *The Revenge* to his children, or such parts of it that he
could remember. I thought that it was the most heroic tale I
had ever heard. My father was at his best with ". . . The lion
lay there dying and they yielded to the foe." I, of course, was
Sir Richard Grenville in my own mind.❜

from Border March

by Sir Walter Scott

March, march, Ettrick, and Teviotdale,
   Why the deil dinna ye march forward in order?
March, march, Eskdale and Liddesdale,
    All the Blue Bonnets are bound for the Border.
     Many a banner spread,
     Flutters above your head,
    Many a crest that is famous in story.
     Mount and make ready then,
     Sons of the mountain glen,
Fight for the Queen and our old Scottish glory.

Come from the hills where your hirsels are grazing,
   Come from the glen of the buck and the roe;
Come to the crag where the beacon is blazing,
    Come with the buckler, the lance, and the bow.
     Trumpets are sounding,
     War-steeds are bounding,
    Stand to your arms, and march in good order;
     England shall many a day
     Tell of the bloody fray,
When the Blue Bonnets came over the Border.

Chosen by **The Rt Hon Sir David Steel** MP, former Leader of the Liberal Party

❛At primary school in Edinburgh our classes used to march out to the playground to this stirring song. I did not realize then that I would spend my life representing The Borders in parliament.❜

from Vitaï Lampada

by Sir Henry Newbolt

There's a breathless hush in the Close to-night—
    Ten to make and the match to win—
A bumping pitch and a blinding light,
    An hour to play and the last man in.
And it's not for the sake of a ribboned coat,
    Or the selfish hope of a season's fame,
But his Captain's hand on his shoulder smote—
    'Play up! play up! and play the game!'

The sand of the desert is sodden red,—
    Red with the wreck of a square that broke;—
The Gatling's jammed and the Colonel dead,
    And the regiment blind with dust and smoke.
The river of death has brimmed his banks,
    And England's far, and Honour a name,
But the voice of a schoolboy rallies the ranks:
    'Play up! play up! and play the game!'

Chosen by **Keith Waterhouse**, journalist and playwright

‹When I was very small my big sister would often come into
my bedroom before I fell asleep and recite the poem she had
learnt at school that day—the rhyming equivalent of the
bedtime story. Requests were entertained—firm favourites were
Sea Fever and Drake's Drum. I was captivated, however, by
Henry Newbolt's Vitai Lampada ("There's a breathless hush
in the Close tonight") which I clamoured for again and again.
Although I was too small to comprehend that the poem is
about cricket (it is, of course, about a good deal more), its
drama held me in thrall. I wonder if big sisters still recite poems
to younger brothers? I fear not—›

90

Epitaph on an Army of Mercenaries

by A.E. Housman

These, in the day when heaven was falling,
The hour when earth's foundations fled,
Followed their mercenary calling
And took their wages and are dead.

Their shoulders held the sky suspended;
They stood, and earth's foundations stay;
What God abandoned, these defended,
And saved the sum of things for pay.

Chosen by **Nina Bawden**, novelist best known for her children's stories such
as *Carrie's War* and *The Peppermint Pig*

❛I grew up during the Second World War, part of which I spent
on a farm in Shropshire. A.E. Housman became part of my life.
And perhaps I was partly drawn to this poem because my
father was a Commander of the Royal Navy Reserves, and
on North Sea Patrol for most of the war.❜

Strange Meeting

by Wilfred Owen

It seemed that out of battle I escaped
Down some profound dull tunnel, long since scooped
Through granites which titanic wars had groined.
Yet also there encumbered sleepers groaned,
Too fast in thought or death to be bestirred.
Then, as I probed them, one sprang up, and stared
With piteous recognition in fixed eyes,
Lifting distressful hands as if to bless.
And by his smile I knew that sullen hall,
By his dead smile I knew we stood in Hell.
With a thousand pains that vision's face was grained;
Yet no blood reached there from the upper ground,
And no guns thumped, or down the flues made moan.
'Strange friend,' I said, 'here is no cause to mourn.'
'None,' said the other, 'save the undone years,
The hopelessness. Whatever hope is yours,
Was my life also; I went hunting wild
After the wildest beauty in the world,
Which lies not calm in eyes, or braided hair,
But mocks the steady running of the hour,
And if it grieves, grieves richlier than here.
For by my glee might many men have laughed,
And of my weeping something had been left,
Which must die now. I mean the truth untold,
The pity of war, the pity war distilled.
Now men will go content with what we spoiled,
Or, discontent, boil bloody, and be spilled.

They will be swift with swiftness of the tigress,
None will break ranks, though nations trek from
    progress.
Courage was mine, and I had mystery,
Wisdom was mine, and I had mastery;
To miss the march of this retreating world
Into vain citadels that are not walled.
Then, when much blood had clogged their chariot-
    wheels
I would go up and wash them from sweet wells,
Even with truths that lie too deep for taint.
I would have poured my spirit without stint
But not through wounds; not on the cess of war.
Foreheads of men have bled where no wounds were.
I am the enemy you killed, my friend.
I knew you in this dark; for so you frowned
Yesterday through me as you jabbed and killed.
I parried; but my hands were loath and cold.
Let us sleep now . . .'

Chosen by **Glenys Kinnock**, Teacher and Educationist

❛This poem still moves me, and it ensured that when I first
read it, at the age of fourteen, I would never have any illusions
about the nature of war. Its powerful imagery and painful
reminder of our mortality have a timeless quality and
transcend any description of the poem as simply "a war
poem".❜

For Johnny

by John Pudney

Do not despair
For Johnny-head-in-air;
He sleeps as sound
As Johnny under ground.

Fetch out no shroud
For Johnny-in-the-cloud;
And keep your tears
For him in after years.

Better by far
For Johnny-the-bright-star,
To keep your head,
And see his children fed.

Chosen by **Bob Holness**, journalist and television presenter, best known for presenting *Blockbusters*

❛The poem was featured in the British Second World War film about flying, *The Way to the Stars*, and as a schoolboy I was particularly struck by its sentiments. Years later I got to know John Pudney and after I interviewed him on the BBC he gave me a signed edition of his book, *For Johnny*. It's still, to me, one of the most evocative of the poems about those turbulent years.❜

In Praise of Peace

by John Gower

Peace is the chief of all the worldès wealth,
    And to the heaven it leadeth eke the way;
Peace is of man's soul and life the health,
    And doth with pestilence and war away.
    My liegè lord, take heed of what I say,
If war may be left off, take peace on hand,
Which may not be unless God doth it send.

With peace may every creature dwell at rest;
   Withoutè peace there may not life be glad;
Above all other good peace is the best;
   Peace hath himself when war is all bestead;
   Peace is secure, war ever is adread;
Peace is of all charity the key,
That hath the life and soulè for to weigh.

For honour vain, or for the worldès good,
   They that aforetimes the strong battles made,
Where be they now?—bethink well in thy mood!
   The day is gone, the night is dark and fade,
   Their cruelty which then did make them glad,
They sorrow now, and yet have nought the more;
The blood is shed, which no man may restore.

War is the mother of the wrongès all;
   It slayeth the priest in holy church at mass,
Forliths the maid, and doth her flower to fall;
   The war maketh the great city less,
   And doth the law its rules to overpass,
There is no thing whereof mischief may grow,
Which is not caused by the war, I trow.

Chosen by **Tony Benn**, former Labour Cabinet member and current prominent back-bench figure

❛War destroys life and peace should be our main concern. ❜

Part 5

VELVET TIGERS AND MEEK MILD CREATURES
Poems of Birds and Beasts

The Death and Burial of Poor Cock Robin

Anon

Who killed Cock Robin?
'I,' said the Sparrow,
'With my bow and arrow,
I killed Cock Robin.'

Who saw him die?
'I,' said the Fly,
'With my little eye,
I saw him die.'

Who caught his blood?
'I,' said the Fish,
'With my little dish,
I caught his blood.'

Who'll make his shroud?
'I,' said the Beetle,
'With my thread and needle,
I'll make his shroud.'

Who'll dig his grave?
'I,' said the Owl,
'With my spade and trowel,
I'll dig his grave.'

Who'll be the Parson?
'I,' said the Rook,
'With my little book,
I'll be the Parson.'

Who'll be the Clerk?
'I,' said the Lark,
'I'll say Aureu in the dark,
I'll be the Clerk.'

Who'll carry the coffin?
'I,' said the Kite,
'If it be in the night,
I'll carry the coffin.'

Who'll bear the torch?
'I,' said the Linnet,
'Will come in a minute,
I'll bear the torch.'

Who'll be chief mourner?
'I,' said the Dove
'I mourn for my love,
I'll be chief mourner.'

Who'll sing a psalm?
'I,' said the Thrush
As she sat in a bush,
'I'll sing a psalm.'

Who'll toll the bell?
'I,' said the Bull,
'Because I can pull,
I'll toll the bell.'

All the birds of the air
Fell sighing and sobbing
When they heard the bell toll
For Poor Cock Robin.

Chosen by **Graham Taylor**, manager of the England Football Team

❛Everybody loves the robin—even though he is a bit of a show-off and a fighter and a scrapper! I've always attracted a couple to my garden. And Christmas would never be the same without him!❜

The Windhover

by Gerard Manley Hopkins

I caught this morning morning's minion, king–
dom of daylight's dauphin, dapple-dawn-drawn
    Falcon, in his riding
Of the rolling level underneath him steady air, and
    striding
High there, how he rung upon the rein of a wimpling
    wing
In his ecstasy! then off, off forth on swing,
    As a skate's heel sweeps smooth on a bow-bend: the
    hurl and gliding
Rebuffed the big wind. My heart in hiding
Stirred for a bird,—the achieve of, the mastery of the
    thing!

Brute beauty and valour and act, oh, air, pride, plume,
    here
    Buckle! AND the fire that breaks from thee then, a
    billion
Times told lovelier, more dangerous, O my chevalier!
    No wonder of it: sheer plod makes plough down sillion
Shine, and blue-bleak embers, ah my dear,
    Fall, gall themselves, and gash gold-vermilion.

Chosen by **Maureen Lipman**, actress, writer (and star of the BT
advertisements in which she plays Beattie)

❲I suppose I like this poem because it was explained to me
when I was a schoolgirl studying Gerard Manley Hopkins. I read
it and found it difficult to relate to until I got the rhythm and
actually felt it take me with it. From the moment the falcon
makes his appearance ". . . in his riding/Of the rolling level
underneath him steady air . . .", you are experiencing his
experience which changes your perception of the poem.❳

from The Jackdaw of Rheims

by Rev. R.H. Barham

The Jackdaw sat on the Cardinal's chair!
Bishop, and abbot, and prior were there;
 Many a monk, and many a friar,
 Many a knight, and many a squire,
With a great many more of lesser degree,—
In sooth a goodly company;
And they served the Lord Primate on bended knee.
  Never, I ween,
  Was a prouder seen,
Read of in books, or dreamt of in dreams,
Than the Cardinal Lord Archbishop of Rheims!

  In and out
  Through the motley rout
That little Jackdaw kept hopping about;
  Here and there,
  Like a dog in a fair,
  Over comfits and cates,
  And dishes and plates,
Cowl and cope, and rochet and pall,
Mitre and crosier! he hopped upon all!
  With a saucy air,
  He perched on the chair
Where, in state, the great Lord Cardinal sat
In the great Lord Cardinal's great red hat;
  And he peered in the face
  Of his Lordship's Grace,
With a satisfied look, as if he would say,
'We Two are the greatest folks here to-day!'
  And the priests, with awe,
  As such freaks they saw,
Said, 'The Devil must be in that little Jackdaw!'

The feast was over, the board was cleared,
The flawns and the custards had all disappeared,
And six little Singing-boys,—dear little souls!
In nice clean faces, and nice white stoles,
            Came, in order due,
            Two by two,
Marching that grand refectory through!
A nice little boy held a golden ewer,
Embossed and filled with water, as pure
As any that flows between Rheims and Namur,
Which a nice little boy stood ready to catch
In a fine golden hand-basin made to match.
Two nice little boys, rather more grown,
Carried lavender-water, and eau de Cologne;
And a nice little boy had a nice cake of soap,
Worthy of washing the hands of the Pope.
            One little boy more
            A napkin bore,
Of the best white diaper, fringed with pink,
And a Cardinal's Hat marked in 'permanent ink.'

The great Lord Cardinal turns at the sight
Of these nice little boys dressed all in white:
            From his finger he draws
            His costly turquoise:
And, not thinking at all about little Jackdaws,
            Deposits it straight
            By the side of his plate,
While the nice little boys on his Eminence wait;
Till, when nobody's dreaming of any such thing,
That little Jackdaw hops off with the ring!

            There's a cry and a shout,
            And deuce of a rout,
And nobody seems to know what they're about,
But the monks have their pockets all turned inside out;

The friars are kneeling,
And hunting, and feeling
The carpet, the floor, and the walls, and the ceiling.
The Cardinal drew
Off each plum-coloured shoe,
And left his red stockings exposed to the view:
He peeps, and he feels
In the toes and the heels;
They turn up the dishes,—they turn up the plates,—
They take up the poker and poke out the grates,
—They turn up the rugs,
They examine the mugs:—
But, no!—no such thing;—
They can't find the Ring!
And the Abbot declared that, 'when nobody twigged it,
Some rascal or other had popped in and prigged it!'

The Cardinal rose with a dignified look,
He called for his candle, his bell, and his book!
In holy anger, and pious grief,
He solemnly cursed that rascally thief!
He cursed him at board, he cursed him in bed;
From the sole of his foot to the crown of his head;
He cursed him in sleeping, that every night
He should dream of the devil, and wake in a fright;
He cursed him in eating, he cursed him in
drinking,
He cursed him in coughing, in sneezing, in
winking;
He cursed him in sitting, in standing, in lying;
He cursed him in walking, in riding, in flying,
He cursed him in living, he cursed him in dying!—
Never was heard such a terrible curse!
But what gave rise
To no little surprise,
Nobody seemed one penny the worse!

The day was gone,
The night came on,
The Monks and the Friars they searched till dawn;
Then the sacristan saw,
On crumpled claw,
Come limping a poor little lame Jackdaw!
No longer gay,
As on yesterday;
His feathers seemed all to be turned the wrong way;—
His pinions drooped—he could hardly stand,—
His head was as bald as the palm of your hand;
His eye so dim,
So wasted each limb,
That heedless of grammar, they all cried, 'That's him!
That's the scamp that has done this scandalous thing!
That's the thief that has got my Lord Cardinal's Ring!'
The poor little Jackdaw,
When the monks he saw,
Feebly gave vent to the ghost of a caw;
And turned his bald head, as much as to say,
'Pray, be so good as to walk this way!'
Slower and slower he limped on before,
Till they came to the back of the belfry door:
There the first thing they saw,
Midst the sticks and the straw,
Was the Ring, in the nest of that little Jackdaw!

Then the great Lord Cardinal called for his book,
And off that terrible curse he took;
The mute expression
Served in lieu of confession
And, being thus coupled with full restitution,
The Jackdaw got plenary absolution!
—When those words were heard,
That poor little bird
Was so changed in a moment, 'twas really absurd,

He grew sleek, and fat;
In addition to that,
A fresh crop of feathers came thick as a mat!
His tail waggled more
Even than before;
But no longer it wagged with an impudent air,
No longer he perched on the Cardinal's chair.
He hopped now about
With a gait devout;
At Matins, at Vespers, he never was out;
And, so far from any more pilfering deeds,
He always seemed telling the Confessor's beads.
If any one lied,—or if any one swore,—
Or slumbered in prayer-time and happened to snore,
That good Jackdaw
Would give a great 'Caw!'
As much as to say, 'Don't do so any more!'
While many remarked, as his manners they saw,
That they 'never had known such a pious Jackdaw!'
He long lived the pride
Of that country-side,
And at last in the odour of sanctity died;
When, as words were too faint
His merits to paint,
The Conclave determined to make him a Saint;
And on newly-made Saints and Popes, as you know,
It's the custom, at Rome, new names to bestow,
So they canonized him by the name of Jim Crow!

Chosen by **The Rt Hon John Major** MP, Prime Minister and First Lord of the
Treasury

❨As a child I enjoyed this poem.❩

My Black Hen

Anon

Hickety, Pickety, my black hen
She lays eggs for gentlemen
Sometimes nine! Sometimes ten!
Hickety, Pickety, my black hen.

Chosen by **Willie Carson**, Champion Jockey

❝The first poem I ever learnt.❞

Heaven

by Rupert Brooke

Fish (fly-replete, in depth of June,
Dawdling away their wat'ry noon)
Ponder deep wisdom, dark or clear,
Each secret fishy hope or fear.

Fish say, they have their Stream and Pond;
But is there anything Beyond?
This life cannot be All, they swear,
For how unpleasant, if it were
One may not doubt that, somehow, Good
Shall come of Water and of Mud;
And, sure, the reverent eye must see
A Purpose in Liquidity.
We darkly know, by Faith we cry,
The future is not Wholly Dry.
Mud unto mud!—Death eddies near—
Not here the appointed End, not here!
But somewhere, beyond Space and Time,
Is wetter water, slimier slime!
And there (they trust) there swimmeth One
Who swam ere rivers were begun,
Immense, of fishy form and mind,
Squamous, omnipotent, and kind;
And under that Almighty Fin,
The littlest fish may enter in.
Oh! never fly conceals a hook,
Fish say, in the Eternal Brook,
But more than mundane weeds are there,
And mud, celestially fair;
Fat caterpillars drift around,
And Paradisal grubs are found;
Unfading moths, immortal flies,
And the worm that never dies.
And in that Heaven of all their wish,
There shall be no more land, say fish.

Chosen by **Lord Howe of Aberavon**, former Conservative Chancellor of the
Exchequer and Foreign Secretary, now in the House of Lords

❠It is a charmingly perceptive reminder of schoolday summers
alongside the River Itchen.❜

Night Song in the Jungle

from **The Jungle Book**

by Rudyard Kipling

Now Chil the Kite brings home the night
That Mang the Bat sets free—
The herds are shut in byre and hut
For loosed till dawn are we.
This is the hour of pride and power,
Talon and tush and claw.
Oh hear the call!—Good hunting all
That keep the Jungle Law.

Chosen by **Dame Elizabeth Butler-Sloss** DBE, Lord Justice of Appeal

❛I was given *The Jungle Book* when I was eight and still have the copy. I read all Kipling's books and loved his poems for the excitement, and the rhyming made them easy to learn and recite. This is the first poem in the first Kipling book I read.❜

Goosey, Goosey, Gander

Anon

Goosey, goosey, gander, where shall I wander?
Upstairs and downstairs, and in my lady's chamber.
There I met an old man, who would not say his prayers,
I took him by the left leg, and threw him down the
    stairs.

Chosen by **Linford Christie** MBE, Olympic gold medal sprinter

❛It was my favourite poem as a child.❜

Tim, an Irish Terrier

by Winifred Letts

It's wonderful dogs they're breeding now
Small as a flea and big as a cow;
But my old lad, Tim, he'll never be bet
By any dog that ever he met
'Come on,' says he, 'for I'm not kilt yet.'

No matter the size of the dog he'll meet
Tim trails his coat the length of the street.
D'ye mind his scar and his ragged ear
The like of a Dublin fusilier
He's a massacree dog that knows no fear.

But he'd stick to me till his latest breath
And he'd go with me to the gates of death.
He'd wait for a thousand years maybe
Scratching the door and calling for me
If myself were inside purgatory.

So I laughs when I hear them make it plain
That dogs and men never meet again.
For all their talk who'd listen to thim
With the soul in the shining eyes of him.
Would God be wasting a dog like Tim?

Chosen by **John Craven**, broadcaster

❛At school, we were forced to learn and remember poems—
but this one I *wanted* to remember. I think it expresses
perfectly the relationship between an ordinary human being
and an ordinary dog—but both think each other is rather
special.❜

The Oxen

by Thomas Hardy

Christmas Eve, and twelve of the clock.
　　'Now they are all on their knees,'
An elder said as we sat in a flock
　　By the embers in hearthside ease.

We pictured the meek mild creatures where
　　They dwelt in their strawy pen,
Nor did it occur to one of us there
　　To doubt they were kneeling then.

So fair a fancy few would weave
　　In these years! Yet, I feel,
If someone said on Christmas Eve,
　　'Come, see the oxen kneel,

'In the lonely barton by yonder coomb
　　Our childhood used to know,'
I should go with him in the gloom,
　　Hoping it might be so.

Chosen by **The Rt Hon Douglas Hurd** MP, Secretary of State for Foreign and
Commonwealth Affairs; **Paul Scofield**, actor, perhaps most famous for his
portrayal of Sir Thomas More in *A Man For All Seasons*; and **Vernon Scannell**,
poet, writer and broadcaster

❝Because it is certainly a poem I read when very young and
remember doing so, and because its theme, Christmas, is a
happy time for children, I'll choose *The Oxen*, by Thomas
Hardy. I think it haunts.❞
　Paul Scofield

❝I was, I think, fifteen years old when I first read this poem,
and its simplicity, and the expression, quite unsentimental, of
a wistful hope for a Christian belief which eludes the poet,
pierced me to the heart. And it still does.❞
　Vernon Scannell

110

The Cow

by Robert Louis Stevenson

The friendly cow all red and white,
   I love with all my heart:
She gives me cream with all her might,
   To eat with apple-tart.

She wanders lowing here and there,
   And yet she cannot stray,
All in the pleasant open air,
   The pleasant light of day;

And blown by all the winds that pass
   And wet with all the showers,
She walks among the meadow grass
   And eats the meadow flowers.

Chosen by **Loyd Grossman**, broadcaster and food lover, best known for rummaging through celebrities' houses in *Through the Keyhole* and presenting *Masterchef*

❛Nostalgically, it is one of the poems my mother used to read to me. Now I am old enough (just) to see it as a splendid elevation of the commonplace.❜

The Tyger

by William Blake

Tyger! Tyger! burning bright
In the forests of the night,
What immortal hand or eye
Could frame thy fearful symmetry?

In what distant deeps or skies
Burnt the fire of thine eyes?
On what wings dare he aspire?
What the hand dare seize the fire?

And what shoulder, & what art,
Could twist the sinews of thy heart?
And when thy heart began to beat,
What dread hand? & what dread feet?

What the hammer? what the chain?
In what furnace was thy brain?
What the anvil? what dread grasp
Dare its deadly terrors clasp?

When the stars threw down their spears,
And water'd heaven with their tears,
Did he smile his work to see?
Did he who made the Lamb make thee?

Tyger! Tyger! burning bright
In the forests of the night,
What immortal hand or eye
Dare frame thy fearful symmetry?

Chosen by **Adrian Mitchell**, poet, playwright and novelist; **John Le Carré**, novelist and thriller writer; **Seamus Heaney**, poet; **Chris Bonington** CBE, mountaineer; **Martin Amis**, novelist; and **Sue Townsend**, author, creator of *Adrian Mole*

❪It made my hair stand on end when I first read it as a boy. It still does, and William Blake has become the man whose life and work is most precious to me—among the people I have never met.❫

Adrian Mitchell

❪*The Tyger* was given to our class not for "appreciation" but for "comprehension", but its hypnotic beat, its mixture of radiance and menace, were unforgettable.❫

Seamus Heaney

❪This is one of the poems which really captured my imagination when I was young.❫

Chris Bonington CBE

India

by W.J. Turner

They hunt, the velvet tigers in the jungle,
The spotted jungle full of shapeless patches—
Sometimes they're leaves, sometimes they're hanging
      flowers,
Sometimes they're hot gold patches of the sun:
They hunt, the velvet tigers in the jungle!

   What do they hunt by glimmering pools of water,
By the round silver Moon, the Pool of Heaven?—
In the striped grass, amid the barkless trees—
The stars scattered like eyes of beasts above them!

   What do they hunt, their hot breath scorching
      insects?
Insects that blunder blindly in the way,
Vividly fluttering—they also are hunting,
Are glittering with a tiny ecstasy!

   The grass is flaming and the trees are growing,
The very mud is gurgling in the pools,
Green toads are watching, crimson parrots flying,
Two pairs of eyes meet one another glowing—
They hunt, the velvet tigers in the jungle.

Chosen by **Len Deighton**, author famous for his thriller and spy stories

❛I enjoy this poem because it is short, concentrating on
description, while leaving the emotion to the reader. This seems
to be a sound rule for writers of stories, news, committee
minutes and business reports, as well as for poets and
critics.❜

W-o-o-o-o-oww!

by Nancy M. Hayes

Away in the forest, all darksome and deep,
The Wolves went a-hunting when men were asleep:
And the cunning Old Wolves were so patient and wise,
As they taught the young Cubs how to see with their
    eyes,
How to smell with their noses and hear with their ears,
And what a Wolf hunts for and what a Wolf fears.
Of danger they warned: 'Cubs, you mustn't go there—
It's the home of the Grizzily-izzily Bear!
      W-o-o-o-o-oww!'

The Cubs in the pack very soon understood
If they followed the Wolf Law the hunting was good,
And Old Wolves who'd hunted long winters ago
Knew better than they did the right way to go.
But one silly Cub thought he always was right,
And he settled to do his *own* hunting one night.
He laughed at the warning—said *he* didn't care
For the Grizzily-izzily-izzily Bear!
      W-o-o-o-o-oww!

So, when all his elders were hot on the track,
'I'm off now!' he barked to the Cubs of the Pack.
'I'll have some adventures—don't mind what you say!'
A wave of his paw—and he bounded away.
He bounded away till he came very soon,
Where the edge of the forest lay white in the moon,
To what he'd been warned of—that terrible lair—
The haunt of the Grizzily-izzily Bear!
      W-o-o-o-o-oww!

He came. . . . And what happened? Alas, to the Pack
That poor silly Wolf-Cub has never won back.
And once, in a neat little heap on the ground,
The end of a tail and a whisker were found,
Some fur, and a nose-tip, a bristle or two,
And the kindly Old Wolves shook their heads, for they
    knew
It was all of his nice little feast he could spare—
That Grizzily-izzily-izzily Bear!
      W-o-o-o-o-oww!

Chosen by **David Blunkett** MP, Labour Party MP

❛I enjoyed the spirit of adventure, complemented by wisdom
gained from experience—by listening before it's too late!❜

from The Walrus and the Carpenter

by Lewis Carroll

The Walrus and the Carpenter
  Were walking close at hand;
They wept like anything to see
  Such quantities of sand:
'If this were only cleared away,'
  They said, 'It would be grand!'

'If seven maids with seven mops
  Swept it for half a year,
Do you suppose,' the Walrus said,
  'That they could get it clear?'
'I doubt it,' said the Carpenter,
  And shed a bitter tear.

'O Oysters, come and walk with us!'
  The Walrus did beseech.
'A pleasant walk, a pleasant talk,
  Along the briny beach:
We cannot do with more than four,
  To give a hand to each.'

The eldest Oyster looked at him.
  But never a word he said:
The eldest Oyster winked his eye,
  And shook his heavy head—
Meaning to say he did not choose
  To leave the oyster-bed.

But four young oysters hurried up,
  All eager for the treat:
Their coats were brushed, their faces washed,
  Their shoes were clean and neat—
And this was odd, because, you know,
  They hadn't any feet.

Four other Oysters followed them,
    And yet another four;
And thick and fast they came at last,
    And more, and more, and more—
All hopping through the frothy waves,
    And scrambling to the shore.

The Walrus and the Carpenter
    Walked on a mile or so,
And then they rested on a rock
    Conveniently low:
And all the little Oysters stood
    And waited in a row.

'The time has come,' the Walrus said,
    'To talk of many things:
Of shoes—and ships—and sealing-wax—
    Of cabbages—and kings—
And why the sea is boiling hot—
    And whether pigs have wings.'

'But wait a bit,' the Oysters cried,
    'Before we have our chat;
For some of us are out of breath,
    And all of us are fat!'
'No hurry!' said the Carpenter.
    They thanked him much for that.

'A loaf of bread,' the Walrus said,
    'Is what we chiefly need:
Pepper and vinegar besides
    Are very good indeed—
Now if you're ready, Oysters dear,
    We can begin to feed.'

'But not on us!' the Oysters cried,
    Turning a little blue,
'After such kindness, that would be
    A dismal thing to do!'
'The night is fine,' the Walrus said.
    'Do you admire the view?

'It was so kind of you to come!
    And you are very nice!'
The Carpenter said nothing but
    'Cut us another slice:
I wish you were not quite so deaf—
    I've had to ask you twice!'

'It seems a shame,' the Walrus said,
    'To play them such a trick,
After we've brought them out so far,
    And made them trot so quick!'
The Carpenter said nothing but
    'The butter's spread too thick!'

'I weep for you,' the Walrus said,
    'I deeply sympathize.'
With sobs and tears he sorted out
    Those of the largest size,
Holding his pocket-handkerchief
    Before his streaming eyes.

'O Oysters,' said the Carpenter.
    'You've had a pleasant run!
Shall we be trotting home again?'
    But answer came there none—
And this was scarcely odd, because
    They'd eaten every one.'

Chosen by **Patrick Moore**, astronomer and presenter of *The Sky at Night*

❝It appealed to my sense of humour. It still does!❞

The Elephant's Child

by Rudyard Kipling

I keep six honest serving-men
    (They taught me all I knew);
Their names are What and Why and When
    And How and Where and Who.
I send them over land and sea,
    I send them east and west;
But after they have worked for me,
    I give them all a rest.

I let them rest from nine till five,
    For I am busy then,
As well as breakfast, lunch, and tea,
    For they are hungry men.
But different folk have different views.
    I know a person small—
She keeps ten million serving-men,
    Who get no rest at all!

She sends 'em abroad on her own affairs,
    From the second she opens her eyes—
One million Hows, two million Wheres,
    And seven million Whys!

Chosen by **Conor Cruise O'Brien**, journalist, author and Pro-Chancellor of the University of Dublin

❛As a child my favourite poems were the introductory ones to the *Just So Stories* by Rudyard Kipling. I remember best *The Elephant's Child.*❜

Part 6

LOOK UP AT THE SKIES
Poems of the Weather and Seasons

from Resolution and Independence
by William Wordsworth

There was a roaring in the wind all night;
The rain came heavily and fell in floods;
But now the sun is rising calm and bright;
The birds are singing in the distant woods;
Over his own sweet voice the Stock-dove broods;
The Jay makes answer as the Magpie chatters;
And all the air is filled with pleasant noise of waters.

All things that love the sun are out of doors;
The sky rejoices in the morning's birth;
The grass is bright with rain-drops;—on the moors
The hare is running races in her mirth;
And with her feet she from the plashy earth
Raises a mist; that, glittering in the sun,
Runs with her all the way, wherever she doth run.

Chosen by **Jill Barklem**, author, and creator of the *Brambly Hedge* series

❛My sister used to recite this when we went to elocution
lessons. There were huge tassels on the sofa, and a patterned
carpet on which I was allowed to play with building bricks. I
was fascinated by the word "plashy", and the idea of the mist
running with the hare. And the sunshine in the words stays with
me.❜

The West Wind

by John Masefield

It's a warm wind, the west wind, full of birds' cries;
I never hear the west wind but tears are in my eyes.
For it comes from the west lands, the old brown hills,
And April's in the west wind, and daffodils.

It's a fine land, the west land, for hearts as tired as
    mine,
Apple orchards blossom there, and the air's like wine.
There is cool green grass there, where men may lie at
    rest,
And the thrushes are in song there, fluting from the
    nest.

'Will you not come home, brother? you have been long
    away,
It's April, and blossom time, and white is the may;
And bright is the sun, brother, and warm is the rain,—
Will you not come home, brother, home to us again?

'The young corn is green, brother, where the rabbits
    run,
It's blue sky, and white clouds, and warm rain and sun.
It's song to a man's soul, brother, fire to a man's brain,
To hear the wild bees and see the merry spring again.

'Larks are singing in the west, brother, above the green
    wheat,
So will you not come home, brother, and rest your tired
    feet,
I've a balm for bruised hearts, brother, sleep for aching
    eyes,'
Says the warm wind, the west wind, full of birds' cries.

Chosen by **Stephanie Cole**, actress

❲At the age of eight it filled me with a delicious sadness, a
nostalgia for the Devon I was brought up in.❳

The Starlight Night

by Gerard Manley Hopkins

Look at the stars! look, look up at the skies!
  O look at all the fire-folk sitting in the air!
  The bright boroughs, the circle-citadels there!
Down in dim woods the diamond delves! the elves'-
    eyes!
The grey lawns cold where gold, where quickgold lies!
  Wind-beat whitebeam! airy abeles set on a flare!
  Flake-doves sent floating forth at a farmyard scare!
Ah well! it is all a purchase, all is a prize.

Buy then! bid then!—What?—Prayer, patience, alms,
    vows.
Look, look: a May-mess, like on orchard boughs!
  Look! March-bloom, like on mealed-with-yellow
    sallows!
These are indeed the barn; withindoors house
The shocks. This piece-bright paling shuts the spouse
  Christ home, Christ and his mother and all his
    hallows.

Chosen by **Lord Healey of Riddlesden**, formerly Denis Healey, Chancellor
of the Exchequer and Deputy Leader of the Labour Party

❛When I was in the sixth form at Bradford Grammar School, a
young teacher introduced me to the poetry of Gerard Manley
Hopkins. I asked for a collection of Hopkins' poems when I
won the school Classical Prize in 1936.❜

The Rain

by Baron Charles Bowen

The rain it raineth every day
Upon the just and unjust fella
But mostly on the just, because
The unjust hath the just's umbrella.

Chosen by **Wendy Cope**, author and poet

‵This was recited to me as a child and I've been reciting it
ever since.ʼ

from **The Cloud**

by P.B. Shelley

I bring fresh showers for the thirsting flowers,
    From the seas and the streams;
I bear light shade for the leaves when laid
      In their noonday dreams.
From my wings are shaken the dews that waken
      The sweet buds every one,
When rocked to rest on their mother's breast,
      As she dances about the sun.
I wield the flail of the lashing hail,
      And whiten the green plains under,
And then again I dissolve it in rain,
      And laugh as I pass in thunder.

I am the daughter of Earth and Water,
  And the nursling of the Sky;
I pass through the pores of the ocean and shores;
  I change, but I cannot die.
For after the rain when with never a stain
  The pavilion of Heaven is bare,
And the winds and sunbeams with their convex gleams
  Build up the blue dome of air,
I silently laugh at my own cenotaph,
  And out of the caverns of rain,
Like a child from the womb, like a ghost from the tomb,
  I arise and unbuild it again.

Chosen by **K.M. Peyton**, novelist and writer of the *Flambards* series

❲This is the poem that most moved me in my youth. I knew it
all by heart—it is wonderful to say. We did the more dignified
poems at school. I found this in the book myself, and loved
it.❳

Ode to the West Wind

by P.B. Shelley

O Wild West Wind, thou breath of Autumn's being,
Thou, from whose unseen presence the leaves dead
Are driven, like ghosts from an enchanter fleeing,

Yellow, and black, and pale, and hectic red,
Pestilence-stricken multitudes: O thou,
Who chariotest to their dark wintry bed

The winged seeds, where they lie cold and low,
Each like a corpse within its grave, until
Thine azure sister of the Spring shall blow

Her clarion o'er the dreaming earth, and fill
(Driving sweet buds like flocks to feed in air)
With living hues and odours plain and hill:

Wild Spirit, which art moving everywhere;
Destroyer and preserver; hear, oh, hear!

Make me thy lyre, even as the forest is:
What if my leaves are falling like its own!
The tumult of thy mighty harmonies

Will take from both a deep, autumnal tone,
Sweet though in sadness. Be thou, Spirit fierce,
My spirit! Be thou me, impetuous one!

Drive my dead thoughts over the universe
Like withered leaves to quicken a new birth!
And, by the incantation of this verse,

Scatter, as from an unextinguished hearth
Ashes and sparks, my words among mankind!
Be through my lips to unawakened earth

The trumpet of a prophecy! O, Wind,
If Winter comes, can Spring be far behind?

Chosen by **Sir Robin Day**, journalist and television broadcaster

Spring and Fall:

to a young child

by Gerard Manley Hopkins

Margaret, are you grieving
Over Goldengrove unleaving?
Leaves, like the things of man, you
With your fresh thoughts care for, can you?

Ah! as the heart grows older
It will come to such sights colder
By and by, nor spare a sigh
Though worlds of wanwood leafmeal lie;
And yet you *will* weep and know why.
Now no matter, child, the name:
Sorrow's springs are the same.
Nor mouth had, no nor mind, expressed
What heart heard of, ghost guessed:
It is the blight man was born for,
It is Margaret you mourn for.

Chosen by **Ian McKellen**, actor and **Margaret Drabble**, novelist

❛I love the serious irony of these lines which nevertheless make me smile. Margaret is presumably in her pram crying her eyes out, so that the poet must really have had to have shouted to get her attention! To the passer-by, it would be a humorous scene.❜

Ian McKellen

❛This was one of my father's favourite poems and he used to recite it over Sunday lunch. It is one of the first adult poems I learned to like as a child and I still find it very haunting. Each autumn it returns to me.❜

Margaret Drabble

When Icicles Hang:

from **Love's Labour's Lost**
by William Shakespeare

When icicles hang by the wall,
And Dick the shepherd blows his nail,
And Tom bears logs into the hall,
And milk comes frozen home in pail,
When blood is nipp'd, and ways be foul,
Then nightly sings the staring owl,
                              Tu-who;
Tu-whit, tu-who—a merry note,
While greasy Joan doth keel the pot.

When all aloud the wind doth blow,
And coughing drowns the parson's saw,
And birds sit brooding in the snow,
And Marian's nose looks red and raw,
When roasted crabs hiss in the bowl,
Then nightly sings the staring owl,
                              Tu-who;
Tu-whit, tu-who—a merry note,
While greasy Joan doth keel the pot.

Chosen by **George MacDonald Fraser**, author and journalist

❛When I first read it as a child, I thought, "Yes, that's winter", and nowadays, whenever the cold weather starts, it comes back to me.❜

The Testament of Beauty

by Robert Bridges

The sky's unresting cloudland, that with varying play
sifteth the sunlight thru' its figured shades, that now
stand in massive range, cumulated stupendous
mountainous snowbillowy up-piled in dazzling sheen.
Now like sailing ships on a calm ocean drifting,
now scatter'd wispy waifs, that neath the eager blaze
disperse in air; Or now parcelling the icy inane
highspredd in fine diaper of silver and mother-of-pearl
freaking the intense azure; Now scurrying close
    o'erhead,
wild ink-hued random racers that fling sheeted rain
gustily, and with garish bows laughing o'erarch the land:
Or, if the spirit of storm be abroad, huge molten glooms
mount on the horizon stealthily, and gathering as they
    climb
deep-freighted with live lightning, thunder and
    drenching flood
rebuff the winds, and with black-purpling terror impend
til they be driven away, when grave Night peacefully
clearing her heav'nly rondure of its turbid veils
layeth bare the playthings of Creation's babyhood;
and the immortal fireballs of her uttermost space
twinkle like friendly rushlights on the countryside.

Chosen by **Dame Cicely Saunders**, Chairman of St Christopher's Hospice,
and campaigner for the Care of the Dying

❛The passage I have chosen was a great comfort to me when
I was fifteen and very unhappy at boarding school. I learnt it
by heart and used to repeat it to myself. I think many people
look at the sky for comfort and I have certainly done so more
than once in my life since then.❜

Part 7

A FIRE WAS IN MY HEAD
Poems of Magic and Mystery

The Song of Wandering Aengus
by W.B. Yeats

I went out to the hazel wood,
Because a fire was in my head,
And cut and peeled a hazel wand,
And hooked a berry to a thread,
And when white moths were on a wing,
And moth-like stars were flickering out,
I dropped the berry in a stream,
And caught a little silver trout.
When I laid it on the floor,
I went to blow the fire a-flame,
But something rustled on the floor,
And someone called me by my name.
It had become a glittering girl
With apple blossom in her hair
Who called me by my name and ran
And faded through the brightening air.

Though I am old with wandering
Through hollow lands and hilly lands,
I will find out where she has gone,
And kiss her lips and take her hands;
And walk among long dappled grass,
And pluck till time and times are done,
The silver apples of the moon,
The golden apples of the sun.

Chosen by **Terry Wogan**, television chat show host and radio broadcaster

❛My favourite poem.❜

The Quangle Wangle's Hat

by Edward Lear

On the top of the Crumpetty Tree
    The Quangle Wangle sat,
But his face you could not see,
    On account of his Beaver Hat.
For his Hat was a hundred and two feet wide,
    With ribbons and bibbons on every side
And bells, and buttons, and loops, and lace,
    So that nobody ever could see the face
        Of the Quangle Wangle Quee.

The Quangle Wangle said
    To himself on the Crumpetty Tree,—
'Jam; and jelly; and bread;
    'Are the best food for me!
'But the longer I live on this Crumpetty Tree
'The plainer than ever it seems to me
'That very few people come this way
'And that life on the whole is far from gay!'
    Said the Quangle Wangle Quee.

But there came to the Crumpetty Tree,
    Mr and Mrs Canary;
And they said,—'Did you ever see
    'Any spot so charmingly airy?
'May we build a nest on your lovely Hat?
'Mr Quangle Wangle, grant us that!
'O please let us come and build a nest
'Of whatever material suits you best,
        'Mr Quangle Wangle Quee!'

And besides, to the Crumpetty Tree
    Came the Stork, the Duck, and the Owl;
The Snail, and the Bumble-Bee,
    The Frog, and the Fimble Fowl;
(The Fimble Fowl, with a Corkscrew leg;)
And all of them said,—'We humbly beg,
    'We may build our homes on your lovely Hat,—
'Mr Quangle Wangle, grant us that!
            'Mr Quangle Wangle Quee!'

And the Golden Grouse came there,
    And the Pobble who has no toes,—
And the small Olympian bear,—
    And the Dong with a luminous nose.
And the Blue Baboon, who played the flute,—
And the Orient Calf from the Land of Tute,—
And the Attery Squash, and the Bisky Bat,—
All came and built on the lovely Hat
            Of the Quangle Wangle Quee.

And the Quangle Wangle said
    To himself on the Crumpetty Tree,—
'When all these creatures move
    'What wonderful noise there'll be!'
And at night by the light of the Mulberry moon
They danced to the Flute of the Blue Baboon,
On the broad green leaves of the Crumpetty Tree,
And all were as happy as happy could be,
            With the Quangle Wangle Quee.

Chosen by **Posy Simmonds**, cartoonist and illustrator

❨Owned a Fimble Fowl, with a corkscrew leg. _Wanted_ to own
a Bisky Bat, but couldn't afford one.❩

Lines and Squares

by A.A. Milne

Whenever I walk in a London street,
I'm ever so careful to watch my feet;
   And I keep in the squares,
   And the masses of bears,
Who wait at the corners all ready to eat
The sillies who tread on the lines of the street,
   Go back to their lairs,
   And I say to them, 'Bears,
Just look how I'm walking in all the squares!'

And the little bears growl to each other, 'He's mine,
As soon as he's silly and steps on a line.'
And some of the bigger bears try to pretend
That they came round the corner to look for a friend;
And they try to pretend that nobody cares
Whether you walk on the lines or squares.
But only the sillies believe their talk;
It's ever so portant how you walk.
And it's ever so jolly to call out, 'Bears,
Just watch me walking in all the squares!'

Chosen by **Bishop Hugh Monteflore**

❛I loved this poem as a child because it struck a chord with me. I was brought up in London and I had a natural horror of treading on the "lines" rather than "squares"—so my progress was rather slow.❜

136

from The Lady of Shalott

by Alfred, Lord Tennyson

PART I

On either side the river lie
Long fields of barley and of rye,
That clothe the wold and meet the sky;
And through the field the road runs by
    To many-towered Camelot;
And up and down the people go,
Gazing where the lilies blow
Round an island there below,
    The island of Shalott.

Willows whiten, aspens quiver,
Little breezes dusk and shiver
Through the wave that runs for ever
By the island in the river
    Flowing down to Camelot.
Four gray walls, and four gray towers,
Overlook a space of flowers,
And the silent isle imbowers
    The Lady of Shalott.

By the margin, willow-veiled,
Slide the heavy barges trailed
By slow horses; and unhailed
The shallop flitteth silken-sailed
    Skimming down to Camelot:
But who hath seen her wave her hand?
Or at the casement seen her stand?
Or is she known in all the land,
    The Lady of Shalott?

Only reapers, reaping early
In among the bearded barley,
Hear a song that echoes cheerly
From the river winding clearly,
    Down to towered Camelot:
And by the moon the reaper weary,
Piling sheaves in uplands airy,
Listening, whispers ' 'Tis the fairy
    Lady of Shalott.'

PART II

There she weaves by night and day
A magic web with colours gay.
She has heard a whisper say,
A curse is on her if she stay
    To look down to Camelot.
She knows not what the curse may be,
And so she weaveth steadily,
And little other care hath she,
    The Lady of Shalott.

And moving through a mirror clear
That hangs before her all the year,
Shadows of the world appear.
There she sees the highway near
    Winding down to Camelot:
There the river eddy whirls,
And there the surly village-churls,
And the red cloaks of market girls,
    Pass onward from Shalott.

Sometimes a troop of damsels glad,
An abbot on an ambling pad,
Sometimes a curly shepherd-lad,
Or long-haired page in crimson clad,
    Goes by to towered Camelot;
And sometimes through the mirror blue
The knights come riding two and two:
She hath no loyal knight and true,
    The lady of Shalott.

But in her web she still delights
To weave the mirror's magic sights,
For often through the silent nights
A funeral, with plume and lights
    And music, went to Camelot:
Or when the moon was overhead,
Came two young lovers lately wed;
'I am half sick of shadows,' said
    The Lady of Shalott.

PART III

A bow-shot from her bower-eaves,
He rode between the barley-sheaves,
The sun came dazzling through the leaves,
And flamed upon the brazen greaves
    Of bold Sir Lancelot.
A red-cross knight for ever kneeled
To a lady in his shield,
That sparkled on the yellow field,
    Beside remote Shalott.

His broad clear brow in sunlight glowed;
On burnished hooves his war-horse trode;
From underneath his helmet flowed
His coal-black curls as on he rode,
    As he rode down to Camelot.
From the bank and from the river
He flashed into the crystal mirror,
'Tirra lirra,' by the river
    Sang Sir Lancelot.

She left the web, she left the loom,
She made three paces through the room,
She saw the water-lily bloom,
· She saw the helmet and the plume,
    She looked down to Camelot.
Out flew the web and floated wide;
The mirror cracked from side to side;
'The curse is come upon me,' cried
    The Lady of Shalott.

PART IV

In the stormy east-wind straining,
The pale yellow woods were waning,
The broad stream in his banks complaining,
Heavily the low sky raining
    Over towered Camelot;
Down she came and found a boat
Beneath a willow left afloat,
And round about the prow she wrote
    The Lady of Shalott.

And down the river's dim expanse
Like some bold seër in a trance,
Seeing all his own mischance—
With a glassy countenance
    Did she look to Camelot.
And at the closing of the day
She loosed the chain, and down she lay;
The broad stream bore her far away,
    The Lady of Shalott.

Lying robed in snowy white
That loosely flew to left and right—
That leaves upon her falling light—
Through the noises of the night
    She floated down to Camelot:
And as the boat-head wound along
The willowy hills and fields among,
They heard her singing her last song,
    The Lady of Shalott.

Heard a carol, mournful, holy,
Chanted loudly, chanted lowly,
Till her blood was frozen slowly,
And her eyes were darkened wholly,
     Turned to towered Camelot.
For ere she reached upon the tide
The first house by the water-side,
Singing in her song she died,
     The Lady of Shalott.

Under tower and balcony,
By garden-wall and gallery,
A gleaming shape she floated by,
Dead-pale between the houses high,
     Silent into Camelot.
Out upon the wharfs they came,
Knight and burgher, lord and dame,
And round the prow they read her name,
     The Lady of Shalott.

Who is this? and what is here?
And in the lighted palace near
Died the sound of royal cheer;
And they crossed themselves for fear,
     All the knights at Camelot:
But Lancelot mused a little space;
He said, 'She has a lovely face;
God in his mercy lend her grace,
     The Lady of Shalott.'

Chosen by **Fay Weldon**, novelist and playwright

❛I chose this poem because it evoked a time and place which
could only exist in the imagination—and told a good story.❜

The Way Through the Woods

by Rudyard Kipling

They shut the road through the woods
   Seventy years ago.
Weather and rain have undone it again,
   And now you would never know
There was once a path through the woods
   Before they planted the trees,
It is underneath the coppice and heath,
   And the thin anemones.
   Only the keeper sees
That, where the ring-dove broods,
   And the badgers roll at ease,
There was once a road through the woods.

Yet, if you enter the woods
   Of a summer evening late,
When the night-air cools on the trout-ring'd pools
   Where the otter whistles his mate,
(They fear not men in the woods
   Because they see so few)
You will hear the beat of a horse's feet
   And the swish of a skirt in the dew,
   Steadily cantering through

The misty solitudes,
   As though they perfectly knew
The old lost road through the woods . . .
But there is no road through the woods.

Chosen by **Peter Barkworth**, actor

❛I found this poem in a book I wrote out when I was a boy, of
pieces I used to recite. This one was good to do because
of the romance and mystery in the second stanza.❜

Turn Again Lane

by Gwendolen Mary Evans

Turn Again Lane, is it there today,
Where old folk chatter and children play?
Turn Again lane? Why, pitter-pat-pat,
The fairies surely can tell you that.
If you feel their bright little wings some night,
Just follow on tip-toe, eyes shut tight.
But, if you are young, and won't scorn my advice,
I will whisper the way to you once, perhaps twice;
When everyday London is hiding away,
You'll find it, I know you'll be sure to, some day!

Chosen by **The Rt Hon Kenneth Baker**, CH MP, Conservative MP and former Home Secretary

❮My sister, who was older than I, had a book about fairies called *Turn Again Lane*. It had a bright orange cover with a blue picture about four inches square on the front. It showed a cobbled street in an old gabled town at dusk with the stars coming out, with brightly lit windows, and fairies, carrying red lanterns made from the seed pods of flowers, running down the street. It had a short poem and I always remembered the first two lines:

"Turn Again Lane, is it there today,
Where old folk chatter and children play?"

This poem was one of the very first I can remember.❯

Kubla Khan

by Samuel Taylor Coleridge

In Xanadu did Kubla Khan
A stately pleasure-dome decree:
Where Alph, the sacred river, ran
Through caverns measureless to man
Down to a sunless sea.
So twice five miles of fertile ground
With walls and towers were girdled round:
And there were gardens bright with sinuous rills
Where blossomed many an incense-bearing tree;
And here were forests ancient as the hills,
Enfolding sunny spots of greenery.

But O, that deep romantic chasm which slanted
Down the green hill athwart a cedarn cover!
A savage place! as holy and enchanted
As e'er beneath a waning moon was haunted
By woman wailing for her demon-lover!
And from this chasm, with ceaseless turmoil seething,
As if this earth in fast thick pants were breathing,
A mighty fountain momently was forced;
Amid whose swift half-intermitted burst
Huge fragments vaulted like rebounding hail,
Or chaffy grain beneath the thresher's flail:
And 'mid these dancing rocks at once and ever
It flung up momently the sacred river.
Five miles meandering with a mazy motion
Through wood and dale the sacred river ran,
Then reached the caverns measureless to man,
And sank in tumult to a lifeless ocean:
And 'mid this tumult Kubla heard from far
Ancestral voices propehsying war!

    The shadow of the dome of pleasure
       Floated midway on the waves;
    Where was heard the mingled measure
       From the fountain and the caves.
  It was a miracle of rare device,
  A sunny pleasure-dome with caves of ice!

A damsel with a dulcimer
   In a vision once I saw:
It was an Abyssinian maid,
   And on her dulcimer she played,
Singing of Mount Abora.
Could I revive within me,
   Her symphony and song,
To such a deep delight 'twould win me,
That with music loud and long,
I would build that dome in air,
That sunny dome! those caves of ice!
And all who heard should see them there,
And all should cry, Beware! Beware!
His flashing eyes, his floating hair!
Weave a circle round him thrice,
   And close your eyes with holy dread,
   For he on honey-dew hath fed,
And drunk the milk of Paradise.

Chosen by **Professor Stephen Hawking**, Professor of Mathematics and
Physics at Cambridge University, brilliant thinker and author of *A Brief History of Time*

❛My favourite poem was *Kubla Khan*.❜

The Mermaid

by A.E. Housman

There was a gallant sailor-boy
Who'd crossed the harbour bar
And sailed in many a foreign main:
In fact he was a tar;
And leaning o'er the good ship's side
Into the deep looked he
When a skimpy little mermaid
Came swimming o'er the sea.

She was very scaly, and sang in every scale;
And then she cried 'Encore! Encore!' and
wagged her little tail
Till came she to the good ship's side,
And saw the sailor-boy above
And a pang shot through her little heart,
For she found she was in love.

She opened conversation, very cleverly, she thought.
'Have you spliced the capstan-jib, my boy?
Is the tarpaulin taut?'
The sailor-boy was candid, he let his mirth appear:
He did not strive to hide his smile: he grinned from ear
to ear.
She noticed his amusement, and it gave her feelings
pain,
And her tail grew still more skimpy, as she began again.

'Oh, will you come and live with me? And you shall
have delight
In catching limpets all the day and eating them all
night;
And lobsters in abundance in the palace where I am;
And I will come and be thy bride, and make thee sea-
weed jam.'
The sailor-boy did one eye shut, and then did it unclose;
And with solemnity he put his thumb unto his nose;
And said 'Be bothered if I do, however much you sing;
You flabby little, dabby little, wetty little thing.'

Chosen by **Joan Aiken**, adult novelist and children's author whose works
include *The Wolves of Willoughby Chase* and *Black Hearts in Battersea*

❛I enjoyed this poem at an early age because I thought it was
funny.❜

from The Forsaken Merman

by Matthew Arnold

Come, dear children, let us away:
Down and away below.
Now my brothers call from the bay;
Now the great winds shorewards blow;
Now the salt tides seawards flow;
Now the wild white horses play,
Champ and chafe and toss in the spray.
Children dear, let us away.
This way, this way.

Call her once before you go.
Call once yet.
In a voice that she will know:
'Margaret! Margaret!'
Children's voices should be dear
(Call once more) to a mother's ear:
Children's voices, wild with pain.
Surely she will come again.
Call her once and come away.
This way, this way.
'Mother dear, we cannot stay.'
The wild white horses foam and fret.
Margaret! Margaret!

Come, dear children, come away down.
Call no more.
One last look at the white-walled town,
And the little grey church on the windy shore.
Then come down.
She will not come though you call all day.
Come away, come away.

Children dear, was it yesterday
(Call yet once) that she went away?
Once she sate with you and me,
On a red gold throne in the heart of the sea,
And the youngest sate on her knee.
She combed its bright hair, and she tended it well,
When down swung the sound of the far-off bell.
She sighed, she looked up through the clear green sea.
She said: 'I must go, for my kinsfolk pray
In the little grey church on the shore to-day.
'Twill be Easter-time in the world—ah me!
And I lose my poor soul, Merman, here with thee.'
I said: 'Go up, dear heart, through the waves.
Say thy prayer, and come back to the kind sea-caves.'
She smiled, she went up through the surf in the bay.
Children dear, was it yesterday?

    Children dear, were we long alone?
'The sea grows stormy, the little ones moan.
Long prayers,' I said, 'in the world they say.
Come,' I said, and we rose through the surf in the bay.
We went up the beach, by the sandy down
Where the sea-stocks bloom, to the white-walled town.
Through the narrow paved streets, where all was still,
To the little grey church on the windy hill.
From the church came a murmur of folk at their prayers,
But we stood without in the cold blowing airs.
We climbed on the graves, on the stones, worn with
      rains,
And we gazed up the aisle through the small leaded
      panes.
She sate by the pillar; we saw her clear:
'Margaret, hist! come quick, we are here.
Dear heart,' I said, 'we are long alone.
The sea grows stormy, the little ones moan.'

But, ah, she gave me never a look,
For her eyes were sealed to the holy book.
Loud prays the priest; shut stands the door.
Come away, children, call no more.
Come away, come down, call no more.

Down, down, down,
Down to the depths of the sea.
She sits at her wheel in the humming town,
Singing most joyfully.
Hark, what she sings: 'O joy, O joy,
For the humming street, and the child with its toy.
For the priest, and the bell, and the holy well
For the wheel where I spun,
And the blessed light of the sun.'
And so she sings her fill,
Singing most joyfully,
Till the shuttle falls from her hand,
And the whizzing wheel stands still.
She steals to the window, and looks at the sand;
And over the sand at the sea;
And her eyes are set in a stare;
And anon there breaks a sigh,
And anon there drops a tear,
From a sorrow-clouded eye,
And a heart sorrow-laden,
A long, long sigh,
For the cold strange eyes of a little Mermaiden.
And the gleam of her golden hair.

Come away, away, children.
Come, children, come down.
The hoarse wind blows colder;
Lights shine in the town.
She will start from her slumber
When gusts shake the door;
She will hear the winds howling,
Will hear the waves roar.

We shall see, while above us
The waves roar and whirl,
A ceiling of amber,
A pavement of pearl.
Singing, 'Here came a mortal,
But faithless was she.
And alone dwell for ever
The kings of the sea.'

But, children, at midnight,
When soft the winds blow;
When clear falls the moonlight;
When spring-tides are low:
When sweet airs come seaward
From heaths starred with broom;
And high rocks throw mildly
On the blanched sands a gloom:
Up the still, glistening beaches,
Up the creeks we will hie;
Over banks of bright seaweed
The ebb-tide leaves dry.
We will gaze, from the sand-hills,
At the white, sleeping town;
At the church on the hill-side—
And then come back down.
Singing, 'There dwells a loved one,
But cruel is she.
She left lonely for ever
The kings of the sea.'

Chosen by **Helen Cresswell**, children's author, whose works include *Lizzie Dripping* and the *Bagthorpe* stories

❮As a child I read voraciously. I came across this poem in my mother's school edition of *Palgrave's Golden Treasury* (it is still annotated in her hand). The poem contains worlds, mysterious worlds, and is curiously haunting in its language and repetitions.❯

Part 8

STUMBLING BLOCKS AND STEPPING STONES
Poems About Life, Death and Being

Question Not
by Adam Lindsay Gordon

Question not, but live and labour
Till the task is done
Helping every needy neighbour,
Seeking help from none.
Life is mostly froth and bubble,
Two things stand like stone
Kindness in another's trouble
Courage in your own.

Chosen by **The Rt Hon Lord Weatherill**, former Speaker of the House of Commons

‘This poem was in my Bible which my mother gave to me when I went to Malvern College in 1934. It was a comfort to me then and I now know it to be profoundly true!’

If. . .

by Rudyard Kipling

If you can keep your head when all about you
　　Are losing theirs and blaming it on you,
If you can trust yourself when all men doubt you,
　　But make allowance for their doubting too;
If you can wait and not be tired by waiting,
　　Or being lied about, don't deal in lies,
Or being hated, don't give way to hating,
　　And yet don't look too good, nor talk too wise:

If you can dream—and not make dreams your master;
　　If you can think—and not make thoughts your aim;
If you can meet with Triumph and Disaster
　　And treat those two impostors just the same;
If you can bear to hear the truth you've spoken
　　Twisted by knaves to make a trap for fools,
Or watch the things you gave your life to, broken,
　　And stoop and build 'em up with worn-out tools:

If you can make one heap of all your winnings
　　And risk it on one turn of pitch-and-toss,
And lose, and start again at your beginnings
　　And never breathe a word about your loss;
If you can force your heart and nerve and sinew
　　To serve your turn long after they are gone,
And so hold on when there is nothing in you
　　Except the Will which says to them: 'Hold on!'

If you can talk with crowds and keep your virtue,
　Or walk with Kings—nor lose the common touch
If neither foes nor loving friends can hurt you,
　If all men count with you, but none too much;
If you can fill the unforgiving minute
　With sixty seconds' worth of distance run,
Yours is the Earth and everything that's in it,
　And—which is more—you'll be a Man, my son!

Chosen by **The Duke of Westminster**; **Will Carling**, Captain of the England
Rugby Football Team; and **Dame Mary Donaldson** GBE, doctor and former
Lord Mayor of London

❮This is my chosen verse. I believe it really does speak for
itself. ❯
　Will Carling

❮Many, many years ago my father offered me one shilling (a
large sum then and certainly to me at the age of ten) if I could
recite *If*. He thought—and I agree—it contained a guide to an
acceptable code for life. ❯
　Dame Mary Donaldson GBE

Isn't It Strange?

Unknown (verse written on a greetings card)

Isn't it strange, that princes and kings
And clowns who caper in sawdust rings
And ordinary folk like you and me
Are builders of eternity.
To each is given a bag of tools,
An hour glass and a book of rules
And each must build, 'ere time is flown,
A stumbling block, or a stepping stone.

Chosen by **Alan Titchmarsh**, gardener and television presenter

❨It's a simple poem but one that has a strong underlying message. Anyone can understand it!❩

from The Rubaiyat of Omar Khayyam

Translated and adapted by Edward Fitzgerald

Myself when young did eagerly frequent
Doctor and Saint, and heard great Argument
    About it and about: but evermore
Came out by the same Door as in I went.

With them the Seed of Wisdom did I sow,
And with my own hand labour'd it to grow:
  And this was all the Harvest that I reap'd
'I came like Water, and like Wind I go.'

Into this Universe, and 'why' not knowing,
Nor 'whence', like Water willy-nilly flowing:
  And out of it, as Wind along the Waste,
I know not 'whither', willy-nilly blowing.

Chosen by **His Grace The Archbishop of Canterbury**

❛The questions in this poem led me into Christianity.❜

from Song of Myself

by Walt Whitman

I think I could turn and live with animals, they are so
    placid and self-contained,
I stand and look at them long and long.

They do not sweat and whine about their condition,
They do not lie awake in the dark and weep for their
    sins,
They do not make me sick discussing their duty to God,
Not one is dissatisfied, not one is demented with the
    mania of owning things,
Not one kneels to another, nor to his kind that lived
    ˙ thousands of years ago,
Not one is respectable or unhappy over the whole earth.

Chosen by **Claire Rayner**, journalist and problem page writer

❛I think it was this poem that made me realize, for the very
first time, that it was possible not to believe in a god. In other
words, it was the poem that confirmed me, even as a child (I
was about thirteen or fourteen, I think) in my very real doubts
about the stuff I had been fed about the existence of a good
god and a benevolent providence. All my own experience up
to that point had made it clear that there was anything but,
and to discover that an adult—and a poet at that!—could feel
the same way and actually say so in a poem, comforted me
greatly.❜

Pied Beauty

by Gerard Manley Hopkins

Glory be to God for dappled things—
    For skies of couple-colour as a brinded cow;
        For rose-moles all in stipple upon trout that
            swim;
Fresh-firecoal chestnut-falls; finches' wings;
    Landscape plotted and pieced—fold, fallow, and
        plough;
        And all trades, their gear and tackle and trim.
All things counter, original, spare, strange;
    Whatever is fickle, freckled [who knows how?]
        With swift, slow; sweet, sour; adazzle, dim;
He fathers-forth whose beauty is past change:
        Praise him.

Chosen by **Dr John Rae**, Headmaster of Westminster School and **The Rt Hon Sir Edward Heath** KG MBE MP, former Conservative Prime Minister.

❬When I was fifteen, the master who taught us French—Walter Strachan—also introduced us to English poetry we had never encountered, including the poetry of Gerard Manley Hopkins. For me it was a moment of great excitement when I read *Pied Beauty* for the first time.❭

   Dr John Rae

❬My favourite poem.❭

   The Rt Hon Sir Edward Heath

It Couldn't Be Done

Anon

Somebody said that it couldn't be done,
But he with a chuckle replied,
That maybe it couldn't, but he would be one
Who wouldn't say so till he'd tried.
So he buckled right in with the trace of a grin
On his face; if he worried he hid it.
He started to sing as he tackled the thing
That couldn't be done, and he did it.

Somebody scoffed: 'Oh you'll never do that,
At least no one ever has done it'.
And he took off his coat and he took off his hat,
And the first thing we knew he'd begun it.
With a lift of his chin and a bit of a grin,
Without any doubting or quiddit,
He started to sing as he tackled the thing
That couldn't be done, and he did it.

There are thousands to tell you it cannot be done,
There are thousands to prophesy failure,
There are thousands to point out to you, one by one,
The dangers that are sure to assail you.
But just buckle in with a bit of a grin,
Then take off your coat and go to it.
Just start in to sing as you tackle the thing
That 'cannot be done', and you'll do it.

Chosen by **Bishop Donald Coggan**, former Archbishop of Canterbury

Psalm 23

by David (Authorized Version of The Bible)

The Lord is my shepherd;
I shall not want.
He maketh me to lie down in green pastures;
He leadeth me beside the still waters.
He restoreth my soul:
He leadeth me in the paths of righteousness
For his name's sake.

Yea, though I walk through the valley of the shadow of
    death,
I will fear no evil:
For thou art with me;
Thy rod and thy staff, they comfort me.

Thou preparest a table before me
In the presence of mine enemies;
Thou anointest my head with oil;
My cup runneth over.

Surely goodness and mercy shall follow me
All the days of my life:
And I will dwell in the house of the Lord
For ever.

Chosen by **Jack Rosenthal**, playwright, whose works include *Barmitzvah Boy*

from **Elegy**

Written in a Country Churchyard

by Thomas Gray

The curfew tolls the knell of parting day,
The lowing herd wind slowly o'er the lea,
The ploughman homeward plods his weary way,
And leaves the world to darkness and to me.

Now fades the glimmering landscape on the sight,
And all the air a solemn stillness holds,
Save where the beetle wheels his droning flight,
And drowsy tinklings lull the distant folds;

Save that from yonder ivy-mantled tower
The moping owl does to the moon complain
Of such as, wandering near her secret bower,
Molest her ancient solitary reign.

Beneath those rugged elms, that yew-tree's shade,
Where heaves the turf in many a mouldering heap,
Each in his narrow cell for ever laid,
The rude forefathers of the hamlet sleep.

The breezy call of incense-breathing morn,
The swallow twittering from the straw-built shed,
The cock's shrill clarion or the echoing horn,
No more shall rouse them from their lowly bed.

For them no more the blazing hearth shall burn,
Or busy housewife ply her evening care:
No children run to lisp their sire's return,
Or climb his knees the envied kiss to share.

Oft did the harvest to their sickle yield,
Their furrow oft the stubborn glebe has broke;
How jocund did they drive their team afield!
How bowed the woods beneath their sturdy stroke!

Let not Ambition mock their useful toil,
Their homely joys and destiny obscure;
Nor Grandeur hear, with a disdainful smile,
The short and simple annals of the poor.

The boast of heraldry, the pomp of power,
And all that beauty, all that wealth e'er gave,
Awaits alike the inevitable hour.
The paths of glory lead but to the grave.

Chosen by **Julian Lloyd Webber**, cellist

❛This was the first poem that impressed me. Its language
spoke of a peace that, to a young boy, seemed strange yet
rather attractive.❜

Edward

by Catullus (Translated from the Latin by Lord Hailsham)

Over sea and land come I,
Brother dear, to say goodbye;
To hear the ancient words I dread
Muttered softly o'er the dead:
'Ash to ash and dust to dust'.
Though you hear not, speak I must
And tell your silent body how
In bitter grief I mourn you now.
Custom's servant, not her slave,
Stand I weeping at the grave.
Take this wreath, as tolls the bell;
Brother dear, a long farewell.

Chosen by **The Rt Hon Lord Hailsham** of St Marylebone

❛It is a translation from the Latin of the Roman poet, Catullus.
He also had lost a brother, as did I.❜

Song

by Christina Rossetti

When I am dead, my dearest,
    Sing no sad songs for me;
Plant thou no roses at my head,
    Nor shady cypress tree:
Be the green grass above me
    With showers and dewdrops wet;
And if thou wilt, remember,
    And if thou wilt, forget.

I shall not see the shadows,
  I shall not feel the rain;
I shall not hear the nightingale
  Sing on, as if in pain;
And dreaming through the twilight
  That doth not rise nor set,
Haply I may remember,
  And haply may forget.

Chosen by **Julian Clary**, comedian and television personality

That Nature Is a Heraclitean Fire

by Gerard Manley Hopkins

Cloud-puffball, torn tufts, tossed pillows flaunt forth,
    then chevy on an air–
Built thoroughfare: heaven-roysterers, in gay-gangs they
    throng; they glitter in marches.
Down roughcast, down dazzling whitewash, wherever
    an elm arches,
Shivelights and shadowtackle in long lashes lace, lance,
    and pair.
Delightfully the bright wind boisterous ropes, wrestles,
    beats earth bare
Of yestertempest's creases; in pool and rutpeel parches
Squandering ooze to squeezed dough, crust, dust;
    stanches, starches
Squadroned masks and manmarks treadmire toil there
Footfretted in it. Million-fueled, nature's bonfire burns
    on.
But quench her bonniest, dearest to her, her clearest-
    selved spark
Man, how fast his firedint, his mark on mind, is gone!
Both are in an unfathomable, all is in an enormous
    dark
Drowned. O pity and indignation! Manshape, that
    shone
Sheer off, disseveral, a star, death blots out; nor mark
      Is any of him at all so stark

But vastness blurs and time beats level. Enough! the
    Resurrection,
A heart's-clarion! Away grief's gasping, joyless days,
    dejection.
        Across my foundering deck shone
A beacon, an eternal beam. Flesh fade, and mortal trash
Fall to the residuary worm; world's wildfire, leave but
    ash:
        In a flash, at a trumpet crash,
I am all at once what Christ is, since he was what I
    am, and
This Jack, joke, poor potsherd, patch, matchwood,
    immortal diamond,
        Is immortal diamond.

Chosen by **Alan Garner**, children's author, whose works include *Elidor* and
The Owl Service

❨When I first read this poem I was six years old, lying in bed,
having died of meningitis. At least, that's what I'd heard the
doctor say had happened, but I suspect that he made me so
angry that I had to prove him wrong, by staying alive. Anyway,
here was something that showed me that poems were words
that would go where other words couldn't, and that this poem,
in particular, although I didn't understand the words, described
what I was and where I had just been. It was the sound that
told. Meaning came later.❩

The Humble Wish

by Arabella Moreton

I ask not wit, nor beauty do I crave,
Nor wealth, nor pompous titles wish to have;
But since 'tis doomed, in all degrees of life
(Whether a daughter, sister or a wife),
That females shall the stronger males obey,
And yield perforce to their tyrannic sway;
Since this, I say, is every woman's fate,
Give me a mind to suit my slavish state.

Chosen by **Sue MacGregor**, journalist and presenter of Radio 4's *The Today Programme*

❛I like the resonances of the final line. It has its echoes today. I didn't know it in my youth; but I wish I had!❜

So, We'll Go No More A-Roving

by Lord Byron

So, we'll go no more a-roving
    So late into the night,
Though the heart be still as loving
    And the moon be still as bright.

For the sword outwears its sheath,
　　And the soul wears out the breast,
And the heart must pause to breathe,
　　And love itself have rest.

Though the night was made for loving,
　　And the day returns too soon,
Yet we'll go no more a-roving
　　By the light of the moon.

Chosen by **Nigel Hawthorne** CBE, actor, perhaps best known for his role as
Sir Humphrey in *Yes, Minister*

❪My father had composed some music to accompany this
verse and would frequently play it, and when I was a child
he very often sang it in his rather high tenor voice.❫

How Do I Love Thee?

by Elizabeth Barrett Browning

How do I love thee? Let me count the ways.
I love thee to the depth and breadth and height
My soul can reach, when feeling out of sight
For the ends of Being and ideal Grace.
I love thee to the level of everyday's
Most quiet need, by sun and candlelight.
I love thee freely, as men strive for Right:
I love thee purely, as they turn from Praise.
I love thee with the passion put to use
In my old griefs, and with my childhood's faith.
I love thee with a love I seemed to lose
With my lost saints—I love thee with the breath,
Smiles, tears of all my life—and if God choose,
I shall but love thee better after death.

Chosen by **Marje Proops** OBE, journalist and problem page writer

❲This is a hangover from my romantic teenage years when I was always unhappily in love with boys who were, unhappily, not in love with me. It is, for me, evocative of the romantic period of my life before I had to face reality in all its starkness.❳

Weep You No More

Anon

Weep you no more, sad fountains;
  What need you flow so fast.
Look how the snowy mountains
  Heaven's sun doth gently waste.
    But my sun's heavenly eyes
      View not your weeping,
      That now lies sleeping
      Softly, now softly lies
    Sleeping.

Sleep is a reconciling,
  A rest that peace begets.
Doth not the sun rise smiling
    When fair at even he sets?
    Rest you then, rest, sad eyes,
    Melt not in weeping,
    While she lies sleeping
    Softly, now softly lies
      Sleeping.

Chosen by **Baroness Warnock**, Educationist and member of the House of Lords

❛Being the youngest of a large family, I was introduced when I was quite young to madrigals and sixteenth century songs. This song was set by John Dowland, and it made me cry with delicious, all-embracing melancholy, especially when I went away to boarding school. I still love it, as it sends shivers down my spine.❜

from The House of Christmas

by G.K. Chesterton

To an open house in the evening
  Home shall all men come,
To an older place than Eden,
  To a taller town than Rome:
To the end of the way of the wandering star,
To the things that cannot be, and that are,
  To the place where He was homeless,
  And all men are at home.

Chosen by **Chad Varah**, founder of The Samaritans

‛When I was a child, the eldest of nine, my father often read poetry aloud to us, and encouraged us to do the same. We also sang carols. I've never seen this poem in print, but I remember my father reading it aloud at Christmas.’

Biographies of Poets

ARNOLD, Matthew. (1822–88) Eldest son of Thomas Arnold, headmaster of Rugby School, who wrote *Tom Brown's Schooldays*. Matthew was a schools inspector for 35 years, but also a prolific poet. He wrote part of *Dover Beach* on his honeymoon. In later life he became more of an essay-writer and worked hard to improve standards of education in secondary schools.

BARHAM, Rev. R.H. (1788–1845) A canon of St Paul's Cathedral. He wrote under the pen-name of Thomas Ingoldsby and the *Ingoldsby Legends*, first published in magazines in 1837, were very popular. Now the story of the jackdaw is his most famous poem.

BELLOC, Hilaire. (1870–1953) Born in France, educated in England. He was such a close friend of G.K. Chesterton that the famous playwright George Bernard Shaw used to call them *both* 'Chesterbelloc'. He wrote a great deal of poetry for children and adults.

BLAKE, William. (1757–1827) Poet and artist. He was always a rebel against society and formal church teaching, and had his own visionary beliefs about the meaning of life and religion.

BRIDGES, Robert. (1844–1930) Close friend of Gerard Manley Hopkins, who influenced his own poetry. He wrote a great deal of verse, but also plays and essays. He was very popular during his lifetime, and became Poet Laureate in 1913.

BRONTË, Charlotte. (1816–55) Famous as an English novelist, especially for *Jane Eyre*.

BROOKE, Rupert. (1887–1915) Young, very good looking poet who lived in Cambridge and wrote with loving feeling of the English countryside. He saw the First World War as a challenging adventure but died of blood poisoning in Greece.

BROWNING, Elizabeth Barrett. (1806–61) Poet, who was an invalid for most of her adult life. Despite her father's objections she married Robert Browning in 1846, had one son, and was extremely happy for 15 years.

BROWNING, Robert. (1812–89) English poet. After his marriage to Elizabeth Barrett, they lived mainly in Italy, for her health's sake.

BURNS, Robert. (1759–96) One of Scotland's most famous poets, he spent much of his life as a labourer and ploughman.

BYRON, Lord George Gordon. (1788–1824) One of the younger school of Romantic Poets. He was always famous as much for his wild life and love affairs as for his poetry, and at last had to leave Britain, in 1816, to live on the continent for the rest of his life. He died, of a fever, in Greece.

CARROLL, Lewis. (1832–98) This was the pen-name of Charles Dodgson, who was a lecturer in Mathematics at Oxford. His most famous work was *Alice in Wonderland*.

CATULLUS. (around 84–54 BC) Roman poet who wrote some beautiful love poetry as well as political verses. He died aged thirty.

CHESTERTON, Gilbert Keith. (1874–1936) a successful journalist, and friend of Hilaire Belloc who wrote for the same magazine, *The Speaker*. He also wrote novels, literary criticism, essays, short stories, as well as several books of poetry.

CLARE, John. (1793–1864) Rural poet, and labourer in the countryside of Northampton. He had an unhappy life and spent much of it classified as insane. He died in Northampton General Asylum.

COLERIDGE, Samuel Taylor. (1722–1840) One of the first founders of the 'Romantic' school of poetry, and friend and colleague of William Wordsworth and his sister Dorothy. Coleridge was also a brilliant and influential literary critic. Some of his finest work, including *Kubla Khan*, was influenced by his use of the drug opium, which later became a devastating addiction.

DRINKWATER, John. (1882–1937) Prolific poet, playwright, actor and critic.

de la MARE, Walter. (1873–1956) Published many volumes of poetry and stories, for both children and adults.

DAVIES, Idris. (1905–53) Welsh poet who worked as a miner for seven years before qualifying as a teacher. His poetry was strongly centred around Wales and the Welsh mining communities.

FARJEON, Eleanor. (1881–1965) and **FARJEON, Herbert.** (1887–1945) Born into a highly literary family, sister and brother Eleanor and Herbert Farjeon collaborated in their writing throughout their lives. When, in 1929, they began to compose the poems for *Kings and Queens*, Herbert said 'Let's have no nonsense about it. The Bad Kings are Bad and the Good Kings are Good, just as they used to be when we were children.' Of the two, Eleanor was especially well known for her marvellous children's stories and poetry.

FITZGERALD, Edward. (1809–83) Born, and lived most of his life, in Suffolk, and very rarely travelled. His only famous work is his free translation of *The Rubaiyat of Omar Khayyam*. Khayyam himself was a Persian poet who lived in the twelfth century.

FLECKER, James Elroy. (1884–1915) He had a career in the consular service, which gave him a love of travel and far-off places. He died of tuberculosis while still a young man.

GORDON, Adam Lindsay. (1833–70) Went to Australia in 1853 and joined the mounted police. A lot of his poetry is about horses. He committed suicide when he was thirty-seven.

GOWER, John. (1330–1408) Known as 'The moral Gower', he was a friend of Chaucer and wrote a great many very long works in French, Latin and English. He was a friend of Richard II.

GRAY, Thomas. (1716–71) Born in London, he lived in Cambridge for most of his life. He wrote a great deal of poetry and, mainly because of the success of the *Elegy*, became very popular. So much so that he was invited to become Poet Laureate, but refused.

HARDY, Thomas. (1840–1928) Mostly famous as a novelist, and writer of short stories, though he himself always thought his poetry more important than his prose.

HEBER, Bishop. (1773–1833) Bishop of Calcutta. He was famous as a writer of hymns, including *Hark! the herald angels sing*.

HERRICK, Robert. (1591–1674) English poet and rebellious priest, who wrote beautiful love poetry. He is said to have kept a pet pig and taught it to drink beer.

HOOD, Thomas. (1799–1845) He was editor of several magazines and wrote much humorous and satirical verse as well as more serious poetry.

HOPKINS, Gerard Manley. (1844–89) A brilliant scholar at Oxford. He became a Roman Catholic in 1866, and two years later resolved to become a Jesuit and burnt all his poems, though he did send some copies to his friend Robert Bridges for safe keeping. Ten years later he began writing again and continued even after he had become a priest. He died, still young, of typhoid fever.

HOUSMAN, A.E. (1859–1936) Scholar and poet. Professor of Latin at London University, then Cambridge.

HUNT, Leigh. (1784–1859) English poet, dramatist and essayist. *Abou Ben Adhem* is his best-known poem.

KIPLING, Rudyard. (1865–1936) Born in Bombay, and spent much time in India, America, South Africa and England. He was the first English writer to win the Nobel Prize for literature. He wrote prose and poetry, and is especially famous for his *Just So Stories* and *The Jungle Book*.

LEAR, Edward. (1812–88) The twentieth child of a stockbroker, he became an artist, traveller and writer. Despite his epilepsy, depression, and the loneliness of his life, he is remembered mostly for his nonsense verses.

MASEFIELD, John. (1878–1967) Trained for the Merchant Navy at the age of thirteen, but deserted his ship when he was seventeen and became a vagrant in America. When he returned to England he wrote a great many books, both prose and poetry. He became Poet Laureate in 1930.

MILLIGAN, Spike. Contemporary poet, humorist and satirist.

MILNE, A.A. (1882–1956) Prolific author of plays, novels, poetry, short stories, biography and essays, but now only famous for his children's books, and his creation of Christopher Robin and Winnie-the-Pooh.

MORETON, Arabella. (Born after 1690—died before 1741) Little is known about her except that her father was an MP.

MORTON, J.B. (1893–1979) Known as 'Beachcomber'. He was a humorist and satirist who wrote for the Daily Express.

NEWBOLT, Sir Henry. (1862–1938) Barrister and poet, famous for his rousing patriotic verse.

OWEN, Wilfred. (1893–1918) The most gifted and influential of the poets of the First World War. He was killed in action just a week before the Armistice was declared.

PUDNEY, John. (1909–77) A journalist on the News Chronicle until the war when he served as a Squadron Leader in the RAF. 'For Johnny' became the most popular poem of the war, and was originally scribbled on the back of an envelope during an air-raid alert in 1941. It was subsequently broadcast, used on radio, and read by Michael Redgrave and John Mills in the film 'Way to the Stars'. Much quoted, it has appeared on gravestones and was spoken in the House of Commons in a housing debate.

ROSSETTI, Christina. (1830–94) An invalid for most of her life, severe ill-health made her give up her work as a governess to live quietly. She wrote many types of verse, fantasies, ballads, love songs, sonnets, religious poetry and poetry for children, but most of her work was tinged with sadness and grief.

SCOTT, Sir Walter. (1771–1832) Scottish poet, but even more famous as a novelist. The railway station in Edinburgh is named after his book, *Waverley*, and his impressive monument sits in the middle of Princes Street, the main street of the city.

SHAKESPEARE, William. (1564–1616) England's finest and most famous playwright and poet.

SHELLEY, Percy Bysshe. (1792–1822) One of the 'Romantic' poets, and friend of the poets Byron and Keats. In 1818 he moved to Italy where he wrote a good deal of his finest poetry, including *The Cloud*. He was drowned in a sailing accident, on his way home from a visit to Byron.

STEVENSON, Robert Louis. (1850–94) Born in Edinburgh, but he travelled a great deal because of his bad health. From 1888 he lived in the South Seas. He was both poet and novelist (he invented Dr Jekyll and Mr Hyde) and wrote for both children and adults. His most famous poetry for children is his collection, A Child's Garden Of Verses.

STRONG, L.A.G. (1896–1958) Born in England, but half-Irish. Poet and novelist.

TENNYSON, Alfred, Lord. (1809–1902) One of the most famous of the Victorian poets, he was highly respected by Queen Victoria and was often invited to Windsor, or her other home, Osborne House. He was appointed Poet Laureate after Wordsworth's death.

THOMAS, Dylan. (1914–53) Born in Swansea, Wales. His career included journalism, broadcasting and film-making as well as writing poetry and short stories. He died on a lecture tour of America, having built up a reputation as a wild unruly man who often drank too much for his health. He had just performed in a reading of his most famous and unique work, Under Milk Wood.

THOMAS, Edward. (1878–1917) An English poet, especially admired for his poetry of the English countryside. He was killed in action in the First World War.

TURNER, W.J. (1889–1946) Born in Australia, but he came to London when he was seventeen. He fought in the First World War, and was later a music critic, drama critic, literary editor, and novelist, as well as a poet.

WHITMAN, Walt. (1819–92) Born in New York. He had little formal education and worked as an office boy, printer, teacher, a magazine writer and editor as well as writing poetry for most of his adult life.

WORDSWORTH, William. (1770–1850) One of the earliest of the 'Romantic' poets, famous for his connection with the Lake District and his veneration for nature and natural beauty. The poet Coleridge was his close friend and collaborator. In 1843 he became Poet Laureate.

YEATS, W.B. (1865–1939) Born in Dublin. He began his career as an artist but when he was twenty-one he decided to be a writer instead. He worked for the creation of an Irish national theatre and wrote plays for it, but his greatest fame is as a poet.

Acknowledgements

The Editor and Publishers are grateful to the following copyright holders for permission to include copyright material in this anthology:

BARBARA CARTLAND: 'To A Car' © Barbara Cartland 1920

CURTIS BROWN GROUP: 'King John's Christmas', 'Buckingham Palace' and 'Lines and Squares' from *When We Were Very Young* and *Now We Are Six* by A.A. Milne reproduced by permission of the Trustees of the Pooh Properties and Methuen Children's Books

DAVID HIGHAM ASSOCIATES: 'Fern Hill' by Dylan Thomas from *Dylan Thomas: The Poems*, published by Dent; and 'For Johnny' by John Pudney from *For Johnny*, published by Shepheard & Walwyn

EXPRESS NEWSPAPERS plc: 'Hush! Hush!' by J.B. Morton

GERVASE FARJEON: 'Henry VIII' by Eleanor and Herbert Farjeon

PAUL GASCOIGNE: 'Just Me' © Paul Gascoigne 1993

GOMER PRESS: 'The Sacred Road' by Idris Davies from *The Collected Poems of Idris Davies*, published by Gomer Press

LORD HAILSHAM: Translation of 'Edward' by Catullus

THE HOGARTH PRESS: 'Strange Meeting' by Wilfred Owen from *The Poems of Wilfred Owen* ed. Jon Stallworthy

JONATHAN CAPE: 'Jim', 'Algernon', 'Sarah Byng' and 'Lord Lundy' by Hilaire Belloc

MICHAEL JOSEPH: 'The Boy Stood on the Burning Deck' by Spike Milligan

PETERS, FRASER & DUNLOP: 'The Brewer's Man' by L.A.G. Strong

JOHN PAUL ROSS: 'Becalmed'

SIDGWICK & JACKSON: 'India' by W.J. Turner

THE SOCIETY OF AUTHORS: 'Sea Fever', 'Cargoes', 'The West Wind' by John Masefield, and 'The Listeners' by Walter de la Mare — permission granted by The Literary Trustees of Walter de la Mare with the Society of Authors as their representative.

All contributors' personal comments are the copyright of each individual contributor 1993.

The publishers have made every effort to contact copyright holders and would be grateful to hear of any case where copyright has not been attributed.

Index of Titles

Index of Poets

Index of First Lines

186

Other great reads ⤳*from* **Red Fox**

Further Red Fox titles that you might enjoy reading are listed on the following pages. They are available in bookshops or they can be ordered directly from us.

If you would like to order books, please send this form and the money due to:

ARROW BOOKS, BOOKSERVICE BY POST, PO BOX 29, DOUGLAS, ISLE OF MAN, BRITISH ISLES. Please enclose a cheque or postal order made out to Arrow Books Ltd for the amount due, plus 75p per book for postage and packing to a maximum of £7.50, both for orders within the UK. For customers outside the UK, please allow £1.00 per book.

NAME_____

ADDRESS_____

_____

Please print clearly.

Whilst every effort is made to keep prices low, it is sometimes necessary to increase cover prices at short notice. If you are ordering books by post, to save delay it is advisable to phone to confirm the correct price. The number to ring is THE SALES DEPARTMENT 071 (if outside London) 973 9700.

Other great reads *from* **Red Fox**

Leap into humour and adventure with Joan Aiken

Joan Aiken writes wild adventure stories laced with comedy and melodrama that have made her one of the best-known writers today. Her James III series, which begins with *The Wolves of Willoughby Chase*, has been recognized as a modern classic. Packed with action from beginning to end, her books are a wild romp through a history that never happened.

THE WOLVES OF WILLOUGHBY CHASE
ISBN 0 09 997250 6 £2.99

BLACK HEARTS IN BATTERSEA
ISBN 0 09 988860 2 £3.50

NIGHT BIRDS ON NANTUCKET
ISBN 0 09 988890 4 £3.50

THE STOLEN LAKE
ISBN 0 09 988840 8 £3.50

THE CUCKOO TREE
ISBN 0 09 988870 X £3.50

DIDO AND PA
ISBN 0 09 988850 5 £3.50

IS
ISBN 0 09 910921 2 £2.99

THE WHISPERING MOUNTAIN
ISBN 0 09 988830 0 £3.50

MIDNIGHT IS A PLACE
ISBN 0 09 979200 1 £3.50

THE SHADOW GUESTS
ISBN 0 09 988820 3 £2.99

Other great reads from **Red Fox**

Superb historical stories from Rosemary Sutcliff

Rosemary Sutcliff tells the historical story better than anyone else. Her tales are of times filled with high adventure, desperate enterprises, bloody encounters and tender romance. Discover the vividly real world of Rosemary Sutcliff today!

THE CAPRICORN BRACELET
ISBN 0 09 977620 0   £2.50

KNIGHT'S FEE
ISBN 0 09 977630 8   £2.99

THE SHINING COMPANY
ISBN 0 09 985580 1   £3.50

THE WITCH'S BRAT
ISBN 0 09 975080 5   £2.50

SUN HORSE, MOON HORSE
ISBN 0 09 979550 7   £2.50

TRISTAN AND ISEULT
ISBN 0 09 979550 7   £2.99

BEOWULF: DRAGON SLAYER
ISBN 0 09 997270 0   £2.50

THE HOUND OF ULSTER
ISBN 0 09 997260 3   £2.99

THE LIGHT BEYOND THE FOREST
ISBN 0 09 997450 9   £2.99

THE SWORD AND THE CIRCLE
ISBN 0 09 997460 6   £2.99

Other great reads from **Red Fox**

Discover the Red Fox poetry collections

CADBURY'S NINTH BOOK OF CHILDREN'S POETRY
Poems by children aged 4–16.
ISBN 0 09 983450 2 £4.99

THE COMPLETE SCHOOL VERSE
ed. Jennifer Curry
Two books in one all about school.
ISBN 0 09 991790 4 £2.99

MY NAME, MY POEM ed. Jennifer Curry
Find *your* name in this book.
ISBN 0 09 948030 1 £1.95

MONSTROSITIES Charles Fuge
Grim, gruesome poems about monsters.
ISBN 0 09 967330 4 £3.50

LOVE SHOUTS AND WHISPERS Vernon Scannell
Read about all sorts of love in this book.
ISBN 0 09 973950 X £2.99

CATERPILLAR STEW Gavin Ewart
A collection describing all sorts of unusual animals.
ISBN 0 09 967280 4 £2.50

HYSTERICALLY HISTORICAL Gordon Snell and Wendy Shea
Madcap rhymes from olden times
ISBN 0 09 972160 0 £2.99

Join the RED FOX Reader's Club

The Red Fox Readers' Club is for readers of all ages. All you have to do is ask your local bookseller or librarian for a Red Fox Reader's Club card. As an official Red Fox Reader you will qualify for your own Red Fox Reader's Clubpack – full of exciting surprises! If you have any difficulty obtaining a Red Fox Readers' Club card please write to: Random House Children's Books Marketing Department, 20 Vauxhall Bridge Road, London SW1V 2SA.